Reality
NATALIE

Reality
NATALIE

KATIE SPARKS

FIREDRAKE
BOOKS, LLC

Reality Natalie

Text copyright © 2014 by Kathryn Sparks
Edited by Nicole A. Bennett
Published by Firedrake Books, LLC. All rights reserved.

ISBN 10: 1-941036-10-5
ISBN 13: 978-1-941036-10-5
Library of Congress Control Number: 2014915922

This book is a work of fiction. Characters, names, places and incidents are products of the author's imagination or are used in a fictitious manner and are not to be constructed as real.

Printed in the United States of America

To the three most inspirational, loving and influential women in my life; my mother, Susan, sister, Jen and grandmother, Bette. Thank you for being you.

Every Monday, I had the exact same mission. I actually timed it once. This mission required the school bus to run exactly on schedule. It needed to drop me off at my stop by 3:53 pm. At that point, I had just enough time to race home before the clock hit four on the dot.

But today, I was running behind.

I leaped off the bus stairs and darted down the street toward my house. I fished my cell phone out of my coat pocket and glanced at the time.

3:57. If I didn't hurry, it would start. Without me.

My legs burned and cramped as I sped up. I winced in pain. *Don't slow down.*

Bursting through the front door, I dropped my backpack and sweater to the floor. I paused for a millisecond as I passed the kitchen.

No time for a snack. I'd rather starve than miss *this* surprise announcement. I half-sprinted/half-hobbled through the hallway and into the family room.

"HeyMomHeyDadSchoolWasGreatThanks," I said in one big rush.

I grabbed the remote and clicked the ON button. The TV screen lit up before me.

There they were.

Allie Marks and Chloe James: simply the two best talk show hosts ever. They were 12, only a year older than me. The *Kidz Konnection* intro music began. I sighed with relief and crumpled to the floor.

I made it.

"Not again, Natalie," Mom groaned.

"Aren't you sick of this show yet? If I didn't know any better I'd think you're obsessed with it…" Dad trailed off, clicking away at his laptop.

Obsessed? Didn't they know who they were talking to?

I could sing the opening tune word-for-word. I knew what Allie's favorite color was (orange), how many cats Chloe had (three – Kit Kat, Mars, and Snickers – her favorite candy bars), and their favorite vacation spot (Disney World, of course).

"Welcome back to Kidz Konnection!" Allie said. *"As you know, we have an exciting, jam-packed show today!"* The audience clapped.

Chloe stepped forward. *"Allie's right, but before we get to that, we'd like to keep our promise and share with all our viewers The Big Announcement you have all been waiting for!"*

I pushed my blonde hair out of my face and sat on the floor, massaging my sore leg muscle. My eyes remained glued to the TV set. What could the announcement be?

"Do you always have a case of the Mondays?" Allie asked.

"Yes," Mom and Dad said simultaneously.

"Shhh!" I said, turning up the volume. "They're about to announce something *huge*."

"A tax break?" Dad said to no one in particular.

"Comprehensive benefit packages?" Mom muttered.

I had no idea what they were talking about, but I didn't have time to wonder.

"Well for one lucky fan that's about to change! First, we'd like to thank all Kidz Konnection viewers for making us the Number

One watched Monday kids talk show this year on the Channel 10 network," Allie said.

My heart swelled with pride. How could I possibly watch anything else?

"And because of your amazing loyalty, we are extending a contest to all viewers in the Lake County area. If you are between the ages of ten to twelve, we invite you to audition to be our guest host on an upcoming Kidz Konnection episode!" Allie turned to Chloe and high-fived her. "More information can be found on our website, so don't wait!"

The blood drained from my face, and the room began to spin. Maybe I should have grabbed a snack. No, this was definitely not food-related. This was a feeling you got when you realized something big had happened. When your dream was within reach.

I slowly turned around and stared at my parents. Mom flipped through a stack of receipts and punched buttons on her calculator, while Dad rubbed his forehead and stared at the computer screen.

"Did you hear what they said? I can't believe my ears!" I jumped to my feet. "This is the best news I've ever heard."

"What's that, sweetie?" Mom asked without looking at me.

My mouth dropped open. Had they really not heard?

"Kidz Konnection. Guest Host. Audition." I barely found the words.

"I think I'll start dinner," Dad said, clicking his laptop closed.

"There's a lasagna in the freezer," Mom called after him.

I glanced back and forth between the two of them. It was clear they had missed the biggest announcement of the day. No, of the year. The century!

"Dad!" I yelled. He paused and turned to look at me, one eyebrow arched.

"The show," I said. "How does this sound? Natalie Greyson: *Kidz Konnection* guest host!" I waved to a pretend audience, fake microphone in hand.

"Host?" Dad repeated.

"What? It sounds perfect for me," I said.

"Just like the time you wanted to be on the dance team," Dad said. "Or softball. And the time you wanted to—"

"—start your own pet sitting club," Mom finished without looking up.

I frowned. "Hey. This is so not the same."

"How?" Dad asked.

"I'm experienced. I've interviewed lots of people before and know the show inside and out."

"When have you interviewed people?" Dad asked, sounding pretty skeptical.

"On my blog."

"Ah," he said nodding. "Well, this is a bit different, Nat. This is on *live* TV. In front of a real *live* audience."

I crossed my eyebrows. So I wasn't born a dance star or an Academy Award-winning actress. I didn't like those things anyway. I loved the show. It would be like nothing else I've put my mind to. This news changed everything. Not only did I have to audition, I had to *become* the guest-starring host on *Kidz Konnection*.

Monday, April 10
Logged on IN A NAT SHELL
(*via Oak Grove Elementary Intranet*) at 6:03 PM:

Hello blog friends!

Move over Oprah, Ellen, and Dr. Phil! Here comes Natalie Greyson, newest talk show host in town!

OK. So maybe I'm getting a little ahead of myself...

However, I've got great news!

4

The best show on TV, *Kidz Konnection*, is having auditions for a guest host spot! Naturally, I have decided to go for it! I wonder what the audition will be like. Maybe they will quiz us to see if we know crazy trivia facts!

Test your knowledge here!

1) What is the purpose of green fuzz on a tennis ball?

2) How many times do a clock's hands overlap in one day?

3) Bats always turn what direction when they leave a cave?

4) A porcupine's quills (they have a sponge-like filling) help it to do what?

5) A sneeze travels faster than how many miles per hour?

6) Honeybees have how many eyes—with hair on them?

I'm a lean-mean quizzing machine! Leave your guesses in a comment!

That's me In A Nat Shell,

Natalie

P.S. Here are the answers! No peeking until you have made your guesses!

1) To make sure the ball isn't very bouncy and easier to control. Did you know that a tennis ball with little fuzz left is called "bald"? Ha!

2) 22 times!

3) Left

4) Help them float on water

5) More than 100 miles per hour

6) Five hairy eyes

N atalie Greyson, you're next."
I was still daydreaming about the Big Announcement
the next day when Mrs. Wayne, the craziest but coolest
fifth-grade teacher at Oak Grove Elementary School,
knocked me back to reality. I swallowed the lump in my
throat and forced myself to my feet. I tried to remember the
tips Dad gave me to rid me of my nerves, or what I called
the Fake Shakes, because of how my arms and legs shook
like quivering Jell-O whenever something embarrassing
happened.

"Take several deep breaths and talk slowly," he had said.
"And if you need to, pretend everyone is wearing funny
looking hats."

Not underwear, I reminded myself, thinking of the time
I tried that and couldn't stop giggling, which then led to
a major case of the hiccups.

Breathe in. Breathe out. I opened my eyes. Nobody
was wearing any funny-looking hats or sitting in their
underwear. Everybody in my classroom was staring. At
me. I sent a quick wish to the Angel of Nerves, hoping she
was watching over me.

I breathed faster. Breathe in. Breathe out. Breathe in.
Breathe out.

It was now or never. I took a GIGANTIC deep breath.

"Amelia Earhart was the first woman to ever fly an aircraft alone over the Atlantic Ocean. With courage and—*URRRP!*"

Everyone stared at me. Then burst out laughing.

I quickly clamped my hand over my mouth. I felt my face burn so hot I bet it could have glowed in the dark.

Robbie Lovelton hugged his stomach and bent over in a fit of laughter.

Mrs. Wayne stood behind her desk. "Class! Let Natalie finish her book report."

My head buzzed and my eyes blurred as the laughter spread throughout the room. I raced through the rest of my report and shuffled to my seat, only to melt at my desk in a pool of embarrassment.

"Wonderful job, Natalie," Mrs. Wayne said. I knew it was her job as the teacher to make us feel better when we looked stupid, but right now I'd give anything to snap my fingers and disappear.

After the very last report was read, the room erupted into chatter. Mrs. Wayne clapped her hands. "Alright everyone, settle down."

Too bad clapping rarely worked. She put her thumb and finger into her mouth and whistled.

THAT worked every time.

Everyone stopped what they were doing and looked at Mrs. Wayne. She grabbed her glasses from the stack of papers on her desk. "Let's move on. Please take out your math workbooks."

I glanced at my two best friends, Kailyn McAllister and Maggie Castlebury. "Psst!"

Both of them looked at me out of the corners of their eyes.

"Did you guys watch yesterday?" I mouthed.

Both of them looked confused. I tried again, out loud this time.

"Omigod, yea! So exciting!" Maggie whispered back. "Best. News. *Ever.*

Kailyn looked confused. "What? What happened yesterday?"

My jaw dropped open. Was she *serious*? "Did you not watch *Kidz Konnection*?"

"Shoot! Forgot all about it," Kailyn said.

"Alright class. Please work in groups and complete pages twenty through twenty-five," Mrs. Wayne said.

"I—Am—Definitely," I said, shifting my desk toward the two of them while I spoke, "Trying—Out."

Maggie sat straight in her chair. She always sat nicely. She was a ballerina so I think she had to. It was probably a ballet rule or something. Even her red hair was always in some sort of cute bun, sometimes with a braid. Today, she wore it in the shape of a bow. She turned my way and said, "This is unbelievably cool. Maybe one of us will get to be guest host."

Kailyn twisted a strand of her brown curly hair around her finger. "Wow, that definitely tops winning the school talent show."

Kailyn won an award in the school talent show every year. She got the musical talent gene from her mom who used to be a famous singer a long, long, long time ago when she lived in Greece.

"So are you going to try out?" I asked her, a funny feeling creeping into my stomach. If Kailyn decided to, she would have a great shot of winning. She didn't get the Fake Shakes in front of an audience the way I did.

Kailyn thought about it for a minute. "Why not? But only if Maggie does, too. We'll have a better chance of one of us winning."

I switched my focus. "Mag Pie? Are you in?"

Maggie popped a marshmallow into her mouth. Marshmallows were her favorite snack. She carried them with her *everywhere*.

"I'd like to," she said chewing slowly as if in deep thought, "but I might have ballet during the auditions." Maggie was the best ballerina I knew. If she wasn't at school, she was at practice. She practically lived at the dance studio.

"Well, that settles it. If Maggie doesn't, I won't either," Kailyn said.

Maggie frowned. "Why not?"

Kailyn shook her head. "It wouldn't be the same without you, Mags. We do *everything* together."

Kailyn was right. The three of us were inseparable. That's what happens when you're best friends. But secretly, I was almost glad Maggie might not be able to audition. I knew we tried to do everything together, but this time was different. This was my chance to go after *my* dream.

"I'd love to," Maggie said. "I just have to check."

"You girls should surrender now," said a voice next to me. "There's no way the show will want another *girl* as guest host."

Ugh. I should have known. Robbie Lovelton is a mixture of conceited/crazy/weird. Nice, but in a foreign, extraterrestrial way.

"My dad knows a buttload of famous people so it's a no-brainer. I'll bet you five bucks if I win, the producers will change the show's name to *Robbie's Raging Ridiculousness*."

Robbie *always* made bets with anyone who would fall for it, even if the outcome might be near impossible. His dad was a nighttime news reporter, so I wouldn't be surprised if his dad had important connections to the celebrity world. But changing the show's name to that crazy title was an insane idea.

"Or *Natalie's Nifty Program*," I shot back.

"Program doesn't start with an 'N'," Robbie replied.

"Network!" Maggie said.

"How about *Robbie's Raging Realm*?" he said.

"Sounds like a video game to me," Robbie's friend Zach Walsh added. The two of them played air guitar back-to-back.

In all of my excitement, I forgot about how many people might be trying out. Especially when other schools in the Lake County area were included, too. Everyone and their cousin would probably audition.

Which meant I would have to thoroughly impress Allie and Chloe. I needed a fantastic audition that would blow away the judges *and* the competition.

TAKE 3

After school, Kailyn, Maggie, and I hung out in our clubhouse—the tree house Mr. McAllister built for us last summer. It was the coolest clubhouse on the entire blue and green planet. A rope ladder, bright pink door, and a sign that read "No Boyz Allowed" were the only things anyone saw from the outside. But the inside was even better. A small table and chairs painted purple with yellow flowers sat in the center. Two windows with lime-green shutters faced the backyard. Mr. McAllister drilled a peephole in each one for us to keep an eye out for any intruders trying to sneak in. The best part was the back wall, which we turned into a giant chalkboard. We spent hours holding drawing contests and playing Hangman. On the floor we spread fluffy vintage pillows, in various sizes, for lounging.

"What do you think of my blog post?" I asked my best friends as I sprawled on a pillow, Kailyn's tablet in hand.

Kailyn came up from behind me. "Are you *sure* you want to try out? Look at what happened in class today. Imagine *that* happening on live TV."

"Ugh, don't remind me." I paused and thought back to this morning's accidental burping nightmare. Goose bumps pricked at my skin. If I was a mess at school, how would I ever help host a show on TV?

"I'm not sure how tennis ball fuzz will impress Allie or Chloe," Kailyn said, taking the tablet from me and tapping the screen.

Maggie giggled. "Well, unless you made a joke about the fuzz like it's actually recycled belly button lint or something!"

"Ew!" we all said simultaneously and burst into laughter.

"Here are the rules," Kailyn said. "It says the audition will be a back and forth interview with a partner, with the judges there to—"

"A mock interview!" Maggie gushed, interrupting Kailyn. "Nats, you would be perfect for it."

I beamed, forgetting all about today's drama at school. Maggie was *so* right.

"What else does it say?" I asked.

Kailyn stared at the tablet, her lips mumbling as she read. "Oh, the usual. Must be a student between ten and twelve and live in the local area, have parent permission, blah, blah, blah–you know, the boring stuff. It's really long. We can all read it later."

I watched as she tapped the screen twice and put the tablet on the table. Her quick dismissal of the rules felt odd to me. Kailyn was the queen of rule following. But maybe they were long and boring. Who wanted to squint and read the fine print anyway, and get a headache? I dismissed the weird vibe. No use in overanalyzing.

"Anyway," I said. "I plan to have my mom and dad sign the permission form tonight."

Kailyn grabbed a pillow and hugged it to her chest. "Do you think you're ready? I remember that one time in first grade, when we tried out for the *Alice in Wonderland* play, you got stage fright, a runny nose, *and* peed in your pants."

I felt my cheeks flush pink. "But that was years ago. I do okay in front of people—until something extremely embarrassing happens, and *then* my Fake Shakes come out."

Maggie stood and performed a perfect *plié*. "I used to get nervous on stage, but I eventually got over it. You learn to pretend the audience isn't there."

I nodded. "With a little practice, I know I can get used to being in the spotlight."

"Too bad this isn't a talent audition. I'd love to sing," said Kailyn.

I paused, secretly glad it wasn't a talent show. If it was, Kailyn would win for sure. "We're lucky we don't have to perform a talent then," I said breathing a sigh of relief.

Kailyn frowned. "Why do you say that?"

I had to admit. It was finally nice to have a competition of my own to look forward to. I secretly hoped she wasn't reading my thoughts. "Well, for starters, I remember when you guys said I sounded like a squeaky frog with a horrible cold during the chorus concert last Christmas."

"Oh yeah," Kailyn said with a small smirk. "But in all fairness, didn't you have a sinus infection?"

I giggled. "No. That's my voice!"

Maggie laughed too. She sat on the floor and stretched her legs into a V-shape. "Are you trying out for the talent show this year, Kail?"

"Maybe. Not sure yet."

"That'd be awesome!" I said. "If you won the talent show, and I won the contest, we'd both be famous!" My imagination, wild as it was, bubbled its way into exciting future visions; me winning the spot on *Kidz Konnection*; Kailyn and me invited to parties with REAL celebrities; our faces on all of the magazines in the checkout aisle at the grocery store; fans begging us for our autographs…

Kailyn's voice popped my far-off dream. "Famous? Don't forget, last year I got second place, remember?"

"Well, if you ask me, I still think you should have won," Maggie said stretching for her toes.

"Hey! Look at it this way." I chewed on my lip in thought. *"Technically*, second place means you're the FIRST place non-winner. So, you really did come in first place. Sort of," I said, trying to make light of the mood.

Kailyn and Maggie stared at me as if I had announced I was dropping out of school. They burst out laughing.

"Sometimes I think your brain is infested with crazy bugs, Nats." Kailyn grabbed a small pillow and swung it at my head. Dodging it in the nick of time, I flung one back at her but missed. It soared over her head and smacked straight into Maggie.

"What the – hey!" Maggie grabbed the plump missile from the floor and lightly thumped it against Kailyn's back, who fell onto another pillow.

"Save me from The Evil Magster!" Kailyn pleaded looking at me with pretend terror in her eyes. She held the back of her hand on her forehead like a damsel in distress.

I giggled and grabbed another pillow. "Don't you worry. I've got it all under control." I made a move toward Maggie who screeched and scrambled out of the way, but in a quick juke move I flipped around and zeroed in on a surprised Kailyn.

The pillow fight continued until a thin layer of white fluff coated our hair and the clubhouse floor. Finally we collapsed in one big heap, laughing and gasping for breath.

"Oops," Kailyn said looking at the mess. "Doubt my mom will be too happy about the pillows."

"It was so worth it," Maggie said. "BEST. PILLOW. FIGHT. EVER!"

I nodded. "Of the year! Of the century!" I added.

"Exactly. A day that goes down in infamy; a day to remember; a day – " Kailyn paused. "Hey! We need to do something to actually remember this day."

"Like what?" Maggie asked. "Take a picture?"

"Nah, something else. Something big." Kailyn looked stumped.

I glanced around the clubhouse. My eyes scanned the chalkboard with an unfinished game of Hangman, the arts and crafts supplies scattered on the table, and a *Just 4 Girls* magazine on the floor. A picture of the hottest new singers, Divine Divas, who recently won the reality singing competition on TV, was splashed on the front cover. As an idea came to mind, I glanced over at Kailyn. She was staring at the magazine too. The look on her face made me realize she was thinking along the same lines. Our eyes locked and we smiled.

"That's it!" Kailyn said standing. "We need a group name."

"Group name? Like a band or something?" Maggie asked.

"Well, something similar. But since we're out a back-up singer," Kailyn said, shooting a furtive look my way, "I doubt we'll make the first cut of *Who's Got Talent?*"

I giggled and blew some feathers toward her. "Hey, it's not my fault I was cursed with a bad voice."

Maggie smiled. "Okay, no singing group. But I like the suggestion. Any other brilliant ideas?"

"What about The Golden Girls? My mom watches all the reruns. I know it's an old show, but it's really funny and I love the name," I suggested.

"But we never wear any gold," Kailyn pointed out.

"Gold can be part of our signature uniform," Maggie said.

"No uniform," Kailyn said. "This isn't boarding school."

"What about…instead of going with "golden" let's go with divine!" I said.

"The Divine Girls," Maggie said. A smile spread across her face. "I like it!"

Kailyn nodded. "Brilliant Nats. It's perfect."

I crawled over to the treasure chest at the front of the clubhouse. "I saw this idea on TV once that we need to do." Opening it, I sifted through the assortment of items. I pulled out a piece of paper and a box of colored gel pens. "Let's write a Divine Girls pact. Then our friendship is set in stone. Written in blood."

"Blood?" Maggie said her eyes widening in horror. Kailyn stood next to her with her mouth hanging open.

I giggled. "It's a saying, guys! We won't *actually* write the pact using our blood!"

Both of them sighed in relief. I peeked at them out of the corner of my eye and used my creepiest, darkest voice. "Unless...you want to, *muah ha ha!*"

Kailyn poked me in the ribs with a pen. "Get real, Nats."

Together, we spent nearly an hour brainstorming our pact. When we finished, I glanced at our list:

The Divine Girls, Kailyn McAllister, Natalie Greyson and Maggie Castlebury, swear (no bad words!) to be the greatest friends FOREVER (until we are old and gray and knitting in rocking chairs). We cross our fingers, toes, and eyes to do the following at ALL times:

1. Be nice to everyone (Yes, including our annoying brothers and sisters)
2. Tell funny jokes until our stomachs hurt
3. Keep each other's secrets No. Matter. What!
4. Be honest (No keeping any juicy details from each other!)

"Ta Dah! Completo." Kailyn looked at the list. She glanced at Maggie, then at me. "Um, so should we do something to make it final?"

Maggie glared at her. *"No blood."*

We all sat and thought for a moment. Kailyn finally spoke. "Should we spit on it?"

No one said a peep for several seconds. Then we burst out laughing.

"Sick, no way!"

"Gross!"

"Yeah, only weirdo Robby would do that," I said. "Let's all just sign our names."

After we all signed, Kailyn put down her pen and admired the paper at arm's length. "With this pact, we're destined to be friends forever!"

* * * * *

Later, I curled up in my big purple desk chair and squinted at the computer screen. I knew I had tons of homework, but I wasn't in the mood to tackle it. I decided to check my blog before drowning in fractions.

Every student in the fifth grade had their own blog on the school intranet. Part of our unit homework was to write whatever we wanted at least twice during the week. This strengthened our writing skills, according to Mrs. Wayne. This was never hard for me to do. Sometimes I used my blog to interview as many people as I knew. You might already say I was a host of my own online show.

I had just logged in when someone knocked at the door.

"Who is—" I began. But before I could get the words out, the bedroom door flew open and slammed against my dresser. The dresser's tall mirror swayed back and forth, but managed to stay upright. My silver Eiffel Tower necklace holder wasn't so lucky. It swung like an old rocking chair until it finally nosedived off the ledge and landed on the floor with a resounding *thump!*

"Chase!" I yelled, leaping from my chair. "You're supposed to *knock* before you come in."

My four-year-old brother stared doe-eyed at me. "Oopth," he said through his lisp. His lips were covered in red goo. "I did knock."

I picked at the tangle of necklaces, now a huge pile of silver and gold spaghetti. It would take hours to pick out the knots.

"No, Chase, you knocked and barged in. You have to wait until I say 'come in'."

"Thorry, Natalie," Chase said.

I glared at my little brother. Normally I would complain about his (and his twin sister Sydney's) childish antics to Mom and Dad but lately that was as effective as trying to change my bedtime to an hour later. Ever since the editors of an upcoming issue of *Children of Today Magazine* chose Chase and Sydney to star on the cover, Mom and Dad fawned over them as if they were made of gold.

"I'll help." He grabbed at the messy pile, but I quickly guarded my jewelry from his sticky fingers.

"Chase, you're all dirty. Go wash up," I ordered, pointing toward the door.

He handed me a small box. "I got the mail today. Mommy thaid it'th from Gramma."

I took the box from his slimy hands and opened it. A shiny bronze necklace lay inside. The best part was the small glass acorn. It sparkled all the colors of the rainbow in the light.

"I love it!" I glanced at my little brother. "I'll be down in a minute."

I grumbled as he scurried out the door. "Little brothers. What's the point of having a door if it can't keep them out of your room?" I scooped up the mother of all necklace knots and placed it on my dresser.

I spotted a little note tucked in the box:

My Dear Natalie,
An acorn has a tough shell, perfect for growing in its own unique way. It symbolizes patience

and the fruition of hard work. Wear this lucky necklace with pride and be yourself; your dreams will follow.
Love you lots,
Grandma B

Wow! A lucky necklace! I couldn't wait to see what kind of good luck it brought.

Tuesday, April 11
Logged on IN A NAT SHELL
(*via Oak Grove Elementary Intranet*) at 5:37 PM:

Great news! My best friends Kailyn and Maggie and myself all created a friendship group. It's the best creation since sliced bread! (I've heard my dad use that analogy once. Always wanted to use it!) And without further a due, the name we decided on is…. (drumroll!)

THE DIVINE GIRLS!!

This group marks an incredibly important day in our lives. Together we will beat all odds! It symbolizes our strong friendship and loyalty to one another.
Nothing can break us apart! Friends forever! That's me In A Nat Shell,
Natalie

Shared Comments:
Logged on IN A NAT SHELL at 5:44 PM

Hail2KailGal: If you were to look up "best friends" in the dictionary, our pictures would be there for sure.

Logged on IN A NAT SHELL at 6:26 PM

MagPie54: I second that! (or third that?) Best. Group. Ever!

Logged on IN A NAT SHELL at 6:42 PM

Robzilla200007: Not in my dictionary! But I think I saw your pictures under "weirdos".

A t dinner, I swirled my smooshy peas around the plate with my fork, daydreaming about the audition. Lots of kids around town were probably deciding to audition to snag the host job. I pursed my lips together and raised an eyebrow. But *nobody* knew the *Kidz Konnection* like me, I just knew it. I had not missed a single episode in the past two years, and even skipped a family dinner to Burger Palace last week just so I could see Allie get covered in slime during the Celebrity Trivia Tournament.

"Earth to Natalie," Dad said in a sing-song voice, his fork paused in mid-air.

I looked up from my plate. "Sorry Dad! Did you say something?"

"What's on your mind, Ms. Spacehead?"

I laughed. "Actually, I wanted to see if you–"

"Chase! Put that down! It's not a toy!" Dad said, prying the tongs from his hand. "Now eat your dinner."

"But I'm not hungry!" Chase whined, launching pieces of lettuce toward the ceiling.

I glared at my brother. Way for him to interrupt when I finally had Dad's attention. With Dad clearly pre-occupied as the Clean-Up Crew, I stuffed the last of the slimy peas in a napkin and carried my plate to the sink. Mom stood at the stove, piling food into containers.

"Mom? Do you have a second?" I asked, tossing my pea-filled napkin in the trash and sitting at the kitchen table. If Dad was too busy to listen maybe Mom would.

"Did Chase spill? I heard him whining," she said not turning around. "Has Sydney finished her dinner yet?"

I bit my lip. Why was her first thought about the twins? I picked at a small rip in the chair seat.

"They're fine." I hesitated for a moment. Was now the best time to be asking? It was worth a try.

"Do you think I have what it takes to be a star?"

"A star? Why?" Mom said, throwing a container dripping with gravy down the side into the fridge. "Are you still upset the magazine editors chose your siblings and not you? Honey, we talked about this. It was nothing personal. They were looking for specific qualities, and Sydney and Chase had them."

I frowned. Way for Mom to remind me. I still couldn't believe my own siblings knocked me out of my own magazine photo shoot audition. Who would have thought two crazed and squealing four-year-olds were what they were actually looking for? It's not my fault those two demons embarrassed me, causing me to get nervous. If only Mom had found a babysitter, I might be the impressive one starring on the magazine cover. "No, it's not that, but – "

"Can someone grab a towel?" Dad's voice boomed from the dining room.

"That's what I thought…" Mom groaned.

I sighed and followed after her, determined to be heard.

"Guys, you're a mess!" Mom cried, wiping off Sydney and Chase.

"What are we going to do with these two?" Dad said, shaking his head and standing. He leaned over and whispered in my ear, "Can't say I tried to stop them, though.

Funniest food fight I've seen in ages." He chuckled and headed toward the kitchen.

I forced a smile. I had to admit, the twins looked pretty silly with mashed potatoes stuck in their hair and all over their clothes. I doubt any ended up in their mouths. But somehow I knew that if *I* had caused this much chaos at the table, I'd be grounded until I was married. These two got away with everything.

"I have an announcement to make," I said loudly.

"You've decided to become the next president?" Dad piped up, walking back into the room. "I always thought President Greyson had a nice ring to it."

"Actually no. But personally, I think my news is just as cool, if not better." I nodded for emphasis.

Mom shooed Chase and Sydney toward the stairs. "Go put your clothes in the hamper. I'll be up in a second to give you guys a bath."

"Me first!" Sydney squealed, running after Chase.

With the twins finally gone, I cleared my throat and took a deep breath. "I have decided to try out to become a guest talk show host."

"Have you?" Dad asked.

I pulled out the announcement from the *Kidz Konnection* website I had printed off earlier. "Remember? Channel 10 is holding a contest to find a *Kidz Konnection* guest host."

Mom adjusted her glasses and looked over Dad's shoulder, her lips slightly moving as she skimmed the article. She raised her eyebrows the way she does whenever she is about to say *absolutely not*. I took a deep breath and cracked my knuckles. Out of the corner of my eye I saw the microwave clock tick over to 6:58.

6:59.

"Well," Dad said after what felt like an eternity.

"Hmm," Mom said.

These were not encouraging sounds. The last time my parents said back-to-back words of "well" and "hmm", I was forced to keep an eye on Chase and Sydney for an entire afternoon while Mom watched "The Sound of Music" in the family room and Dad went golfing. Every time a song came on, Mom would sing at the top of her lungs. If the "hills came alive" once more, I was going to puke.

I drummed my fingers on the table, glancing at Mom and Dad as they perused the piece of paper. Maybe if I stared long and hard enough, I could somehow use mind control to force them to say "yes".

But, mind control is not one of my talents.

Finally, Dad looked at Mom. Mom looked at Dad. I swear they have some sort of secret language that only the two of them can understand. It has something to do with their eyes. I think it's something that happens once you get married.

"This is a pretty big role for someone your age," Dad said.

"Well, yes but actually…"

"I don't know," Mom said, gathering her hair into a messy ponytail. "I'm sure there will be tons of kids trying out. I wouldn't want you to be too disappointed if you didn't get it."

My jaw dropped open. Was she kidding? I was SO going to get this role even if I had to do crazy things like stand on my hands, blow a bubble twice as large as Chase's head, hula hoop upside down with fifty hoola hoops, or break dance for a whole day. Heck, I'd kiss Chase's gross, sock-boogered feet if it meant I'd get to be guest host.

"Listen. I know I was upset about the magazine shoot, but this is *Kidz Konnection*! It doesn't even compare. I would *die* if I got a chance to be on their show." I clasped my hands together, squeezing them so hard the blood rushed to the ends of my fingertips.

Dad eyed me wearily, but a tiny smile tugged at the corner of his lips. "Something tells me we have heard that before." He rubbed the back of his neck. "Maybe your Mom and I could give it some thought." He winked at me.

Mom sighed. "When exactly is this audition being held?"

My heart leaped into my throat and my skin tingled in excitement. "Saturday the 22nd."

A shadow of recognition swept over Mom's face as soon as the words left my mouth. I bit my lip hoping I was just assuming things.

"Why do I think that's…." she mumbled, heading into the kitchen. She returned a second later, her face hidden behind the family calendar.

"Just what I thought." Mom flipped the calendar sheet down. "It's the same day as the twins' photo shoot. The shoot has been changing dates so often, I can't keep it straight anymore."

My breath caught in my throat. "Well, both of you don't have to go to the shoot, right?"

"Actually, they'd like us all there," Mom replied. "To get a family snapshot for a blurb on the inside cover."

My jaw dropped open. Was she actually telling me that not only did I have to miss the try out, but I had to endure the photo shoot with my siblings, too?

Mom's muffled cell phone interrupted the conversation.

"Oh no. Where's my purse? It could be the PR rep calling. If they change one more thing…" Mom muttered as she skittered her way to the hall.

I glanced at Dad. "Dad. I *cannot* miss this tryout."

He looked at me with sad eyes. "I'm sorry, Natalie, but you heard your Mom. They want all of us there. "

I picked at one of my fingernails and fought hard to keep the tears from spilling over. "But this host job means everything to me," I said. "How can I not try?"

"There'll be other opportunities, I promise," he said. The contest announcement slipped to the ground as he stood and headed toward the stairs. "Now. Looks like your Mom is busy. Want to come help me give those two rascals a bath?"

And watch him ooh and ahh over the twins making the World's Biggest soap bubble? I'd rather fish my cold peas from the trash and eat them one by one *without* plugging my nose.

I stared at the paper on the ground through watery eyes. Dad tromped up the stairs without waiting for my answer.

* * * * *

The next morning, I woke up feeling like a zombie. If my mood didn't prove it, the fact that my hair poked out in eighteen different directions did. Mom and Dad's Big "No" put a pit deep into my gut. This was my *dream* job. I knew I had to audition, some way or another.

After getting dressed (with my new lucky acorn necklace), I slid into my purple chair, turned on my computer, and opened the Compose window on my blog:

Wednesday, April 12
Logged on IN A NAT SHELL
(*via Oak Grove Elementary Intranet*) at 7:02 AM:

Hello blog friends,
  So I'll give you one guess on who has decided to audition for the guest host job? Give up?
  ME!!
  I couldn't be more excited to possibly become part of my favorite show ever! Winning would be a dream come true! My dream would become a reality! The audition is in exactly 10 days. Any comments/advice/tips are welcome!
  That's me In A Nat Shell,
                    Natalie

I didn't have the courage to broadcast that I wasn't allowed to tryout. Everyone at school (okay, well at least my classroom) knew this was my favorite show. What would they think if I didn't audition? They were probably expecting me to. How could I disappoint them?

I knew lying was wrong, but Mom and Dad never read my blog, especially now that they were so preoccupied with the twins. Maybe if they checked up on me more often they would understand how serious I was about this opportunity. They would see how talented I was, just like Allie and Chloe were sure to see.

I paused the cursor over the "Post" button. But since Mom and Dad would never see this, what would be the problem? (Besides maybe having to change the look of my name to Nat-a-Lie.)

I glanced over at a picture of Maggie, Kailyn, and me during the Roller Thunder Skate-A-Thon last year. The pit I had in my stomach earlier now felt as big as a bowling ball. If I told everyone that I was allowed to try out, I'd be lying. And lying would mean breaking Rule 4 of our new Divine Girls pact: *Be honest.* Could I knowingly break a rule so soon after making the promise?

Mom's voice floated up from downstairs. "Natalie, come down for breakfast!"

But if I could prove to Mom and Dad how important this was to me, they'd understand, and everything would work out. I rubbed the acorn charm for good luck.

And maybe, just maybe...*I'd win.*
Click.

I closed my laptop and flung my backpack over my shoulder. Downstairs, Sydney and Chase were already at the table stirring their cereal in their daily breakfast race. I giggled as milk sloshed over the sides and Mom scrambled to mop up the mess.

"Typical morning in the Greyson house, huh?" I asked.

Mom laughed but it sounded forced. "You got it."

I rummaged through the fridge and took out a carton of yogurt. Ripping off the top, I grabbed a spoon and finished off my breakfast in four quick bites. I threw the empty carton in the trash and swiped a banana off the counter.

Mom sat and wiped her forehead, beads of sweat glistening off her nose. "Not even 7:30 yet and I'm exhausted."

"Listen, Mom. I was thinking." I picked at my banana peel. I knew Dad wasn't convinced but maybe Mom would be easier to sway. "I know how important it is for the entire family to be at the photo shoot, but maybe I can go during the next shoot? My audition is only one day so if you let me go –"

Mom's head drooped as she leaned into the palm of her hand, her elbow propped up on the table. The soft rumble of snoring echoed through the room. Sydney and Chase glanced up and giggled.

"Mom?" I asked.

"Shhh! Mommy's sleeping," Sydney said.

Sighing, I walked over toward the table. I gently shook Mom's shoulder.

"What? Where am I?" Mom popped out of her seat.

"You fell asleep, Mom," I said. "I was just saying that if you let me –"

"I fell asleep? What time is it? Oh gosh, we're going to be late." She grabbed her purse from the back of the kitchen chair and shooed the twins toward the hall. "Let's go. Get your shoes on."

I grabbed my lunch from the fridge and followed them out the door. Shoving my arms through my jacket, I couldn't help but wonder if she remembered I was part of the family, too.

TAKE 5

"Alright class, I have an announcement to make." Mrs. Wayne rummaged around her desk, sending papers flying to the floor. "Gee winnegers, silly me!"

I called her desk the "Black Hole"; everything got lost in piles and piles of paper. Mrs. Wayne *always* lost what she was looking for, and if she did find it, by then it was too late.

Mom said Mrs. Wayne was from the south. I think Tennessee or maybe Georgia. She said things all the time like "Oh Lordy" and "How y'all doing?" Her accent was super cool, too. You heard it when she told kids not to run in the hall or "Hey now, y'all sit, please."

A square piece of paper landed on my desk. Next to me, Maggie pointed.

I glanced around to make sure no spies were looking before unfolding it:

> I saw on your blog you decided to audition!
> That's awesome! If one of the Divine Girls
> wins, that is awesome-tastic!!

Boy, was she fast. I just posted my news this morning.

"Class, today we are going to begin our Out-of-the-Box report," Mrs. Wayne said, putting on her glasses. "Everyone will receive a specific topic. Because it's considered 'out-of-the-box', y'all should be creative on how you present your findings. On the day of your presentation, y'all will have fifteen minutes to inform the class on what you learned. They will be due in two weeks."

I thought about my blog post. Maybe I should tell Maggie and Kailyn about my parents' decision. They have always been supportive and understanding friends, so why wouldn't they be now? Besides, if I told them to keep it a secret, they would. Then I wouldn't be breaking Rule 4 of our pact after all. At least not with them. We'd probably join forces, and they'd help me figure out a way to persuade my parents to let me audition *and* help me practice so I aced the audition with flying colors!

Mrs. Wayne continued. "I'll assign partners for the project this afternoon. Each of you will work on one segment of it for an individual grade, and another to be scored based on your group presentation. Alright. Let's jump back into math! Please take out your long division worksheets."

Placing my homework on my desk, I pulled a pencil out of my glittery purple case and headed toward the electronic sharpener. Robbie beat me to it.

"Hey, Natalie," Robbie said. "What's shakin' bacon?"

"Excuse me?" I furtively swiped at my nose hoping it wasn't covered in grease.

I waited and waited while the machine devoured Robbie's pencil. It would be a stub if he didn't watch it. Kailyn sauntered over and nudged him out of the way.

"Hey!" he yelled.

"Sorry," Kailyn said with a smirk. "Guess I didn't see you there."

"You couldn't miss seeing me if you tried, McAllister," Robbie said.

Kailyn rolled her eyes. "Please. Spare me the Everybody-Needs-A-Piece-of-Robbie talk. I'd like to keep my breakfast down."

Robbie raised his hands in defeat mode. "You got it, miss. Wouldn't want to possibly make a potential star like you toss your cookies."

I glanced from Kailyn to Robbie. *Star?*

"That's incredibly revolting, Robbie," Kailyn said and turned her attention to me. "I was thinking more about The Divine Girls and our pact and—"

"What did you say?" Robbie interrupted. "Divine *Hurls*? Wait for it! Here comes *my* breakfast!" He clutched his stomach and pretended to throw up. "Gotta go's, potatoes." He slithered back to his desk.

"Robbie can be such a geek-a-zoid," Kailyn said. "What's with the food talk all the time?"

"What did he mean about you being a star?" A thought suddenly occurred to me. "Hey, are you trying out for the talent show after all?"

Kailyn's cheeks flushed and she flippantly waved a hand in the air. "Oh, you know Robbie. Always talking like he knows everything. Just because his dad reports the news on TV doesn't mean he knows everyone's business."

Mrs. Wayne clapped her hands. No change. She whistled, and finally everyone stopped talking.

I frowned. What "business" was she talking about? If she was trying out for the talent show, why didn't she just tell me?

Once back at my desk, I scribbled a response back to Maggie:

Secret Divine Girls meeting during recess!
At our spot outside. It's important.
Pass it on to Kailyn.

I folded the note into a neat triangle and flipped it back to Maggie when Mrs. Wayne wasn't looking.

Even though I found it hard to tell the truth to my own best friends, a nagging feeling told me I wasn't the only one in the group thinking this way. As a best friend, it was my job to encourage them to go after their dreams. So then why was Kailyn holding back on letting us know about the talent show? I *had* to get to the bottom of this.

* * * * *

"Our first secret Divine Girls meeting! How awesome is this!" Kailyn exclaimed as we found our spot outside near the school garden.

Maggie nodded. "I've been looking forward to it all morning." She paused and looked toward me. "Why did you call it? Don't tell me. You finally got a dog!"

I laughed. "I wish! Doubt I'll ever get one. Mom still thinks she'll end up taking care of it, and Dad thinks it will eat all of his golf balls. Go figure."

"So what's up?" Kailyn asked.

"Well....it's about the *Kidz Konnection* audition." I looked around, glad I had their full attention. I needed to confide in them. "I told my parents last night about it, and…"

Kailyn nodded enthusiastically. "You're trying out! I know, I saw your blog. And while we are on the subject of trying out–"

"I knew it!" I said.

"Huh?" Kailyn said. "Knew what?"

"That you're trying out for the talent show. You were acting strange around Robbie earlier, and well, come on, since we're best friends I sensed something was up. Why didn't you tell us sooner?"

Maggie looked confused. "Wait. Kail, you're trying out for the talent show? I thought you told me you want to sign up to audition for the guest host."

Any feeling I had in my legs quickly disappeared as soon as I heard this. Kailyn was trying out for *Kidz Konnection*?

"What about the talent show?" I said.

"I decided not to this year," Kailyn said. "The *Kidz Konnection* audition sounds like fun. And it's different."

I tried to understand what was going through my head. "But wait. This morning with Robbie. Is that what he was talking about?"

"Well I didn't tell him, if that's what you're thinking. I wouldn't do that. He probably over heard me talking to Maggie or something."

"But you don't really know the show. Why would you try out?"

"I don't need to know every itty bitty detail to audition," Kailyn replied. "No big deal."

How could Kailyn downplay it like it was another item on her To Do List? This wasn't *any* opportunity. It was a chance to shine. To be on TV. Next to Allie and Chloe.

All of a sudden, I felt angry. This was *my* dream. Why would Kailyn come in and try to steal it?

"It is a big deal. How would you feel if I tried out for the talent show?" I asked.

Kailyn shrugged. "I wouldn't mind at all."

I stared at my best friend. "You're only saying that because you think you'd win."

Kailyn feigned surprise. I knew that by the way she held her Drama Queen hand to her heart. "Not true," she said. "You'd have every chance of winning as I would."

"Oh really? It must have been some other friend who pointed out my Fake Shakes or my squeaky frog voice the other day," I retorted.

"Actually, I think you brought them up," interrupted Maggie.

I glared at her. She shrugged. "Sorry Nats, but it's true."

I paused and tried to calm down. "Kailyn, you can't," I finally said through gritted teeth.

Kailyn crossed her arms in defense. "You don't *own* the competition, Natalie. I can try out if I want to." Maybe it was her stance or the way she stared right through me, but I knew without a shred of doubt she was not going to change her mind.

A chilling realization hit me straight in the stomach and traveled down my spine. With Kailyn trying out, no way would I now admit to *not* being allowed to.

I had to think of what to say. To make her believe she actually had a real competitor, unlike the talent show every year. She was right. I may not own the competition, but this was my territory. Not hers. I *loved* the show. She only *liked* it.

Small lies were becoming a habit, I realized, as another one bubbled at my throat, and inched its way up. I couldn't stop it. Before I knew it, it spilled from my mouth like Liar Vomit.

"Fine. I guess I can't stop you. But once I meet Allie *before* the audition, she'll know right away I should be the next guest host." I crossed my arms to match Kailyn's. Both she and Maggie looked at me as if I had said I was about to drink blood vampire style.

"How would you get to see her?" Kailyn asked.

"Magicians can't reveal their secrets, and I'm afraid I can't either," I said.

"Natalie, if it's true, why didn't you tell us? Or put it on your blog? This is the most exciting news ever!" Maggie squealed. "Maybe we can all meet her!"

I shook my head. In all honesty, I had no idea how I would meet her. I had zero connections to the celebrity world. "It's supposed to be on the down low." Five minutes ago, I was ready to confide in my two best friends about not being allowed to audition, and here I was lying to them about meeting the show's host!

The recess bell rang, and the three of us headed toward the school doors. I thought about the pact, and how the honesty part was apparently the hardest to keep, even though as best friends it should have been the easiest.

As I wondered how I got into this mess, an even bigger thought entered my mind: How was I going to get *out* of it?

TAKE 6

Kailyn's news stuck with me through lunch and even through our history lesson. It was going to be hard enough to compete against the other kids auditioning, let alone my best friend.

Mrs. Wayne stood at her desk talking to a bunch of students. "Holy smokes, look at the time!" She waved her hands, her bracelets jingling, and shooed away the crowd.

"Like I said earlier, I will be assigning partners for your project. In order for y'all to truly have an "out-of-the-box" experience, y'all need to work with people you do not know too well." She shuffled a bunch of papers around on her desk. Her loud whoop made me jump in my seat.

"Right here on my head the whole time," she said as she placed a pair of thin green-rimmed glasses squarely on her nose.

"Alright, where were we…ah, yes! I have the list right here. Once I finish reading, find your partners, come and get your topic from me, and start brainstorming until the bell rings."

I *love* group projects. Too bad we couldn't pick who we got to work with. As she read off the names, I quickly looked around the room, wondering who I might be paired with. Emma Hamilton sat next to me chewing on her pencil. Dark teeth marks dotted most of it. Ick! This is why I never borrowed any pencils from her. But she might be a decent partner. Behind me sat Chris Meyer who was super quiet and an awesome student. I know this simply because every time Mrs. Wayne had us pass back our spelling and math tests, he always had a big fat A+ at the top of his paper. I bet he would make a great partner!

I didn't have to look to my left to know someone was staring at me. It felt like laser beams traveling through my head. I wrinkled my nose. Focusing on Mrs. Wayne, I refused to turn my head.

She rattled off names. "…Karen Nelson and Maggie Castlebury, Brett Darren and Jeremy Benson, and, last but not least, Natalie Greyson…"

I squeezed my eyes shut.

"…and Robbie Lovelton." Mrs. Wayne smiled at the class. "Chop chop! Get in your groups."

Robbie? I forced my eyes to look over. He grinned at me, his teeth full of (ew!) whatever yellow and green gunk he ate for lunch. Leave it to me to have the worst luck today.

Robbie shoved his hand into his jeans pocket, unwrapped a piece of gum and flicked the crumpled wrapper at me. I dodged the flying missile just in time.

"So. Here's what's going to happen," Robbie said, chomping on his wad of gum. "It's a great plan, too."

I glared at him. Since when did Robbie ever have a well thought out plan? The smell of mint was starting to make my head feel weird. Or maybe I was still woozy from the laser beams.

"You do the research, I tell you if it's good, and then we turn it in. Finito!" He pumped his fist into the air.

"Me? Do all the work?" I shook my head. "Fat chance. We're partners on this so we need to work *to-ge-ther*." I shuddered. Saying "we" and "together" in the same sentence wasn't cool.

"Ha!" Flecks of spit flew out of Robbie's mouth. I tried to dodge them, but it was too late. A shower of spit landed on my arm.

"Ew, gross Robbie." I got up and grabbed a tissue from Mrs. Wayne's desk.

"Hiya, Natalie. You here for your topic?" she said, grabbing a bowl filled with small paper slips. "Go on, give it a whirl." Mrs. Wayne smiled and twirled the bowl around. A little bit of her red lipstick stained her two front teeth, reminding me of Grams. When that would happen to Grams, I'd try to tell her, and she would laugh until tears filled her eyes.

"Your grandma's getting old, my dear. The eyes don't want to work anymore," she'd say. I wondered what Mrs. Wayne's excuse was. Maybe she didn't have a mirror. Or maybe she didn't mind having lipstick on her teeth.

I shuffled my hand around in the bowl and chose a slip. *Fear.*

"Fear it is," Mrs. Wayne shouted. She grabbed a feathery pen from her cup and scribbled it in her book. I walked back to my desk, wondering what we could do as a report for fear. As soon as I sat, Maggie ran over.

"What's your topic, Nats?"

"Fear, what's yours?

"Competition. Love it! I can think of so many ideas for this!" Maggie leaned in and whispered, "Sorry you're stuck with Stink-O-Rob-O."

I shrugged. Nothing I could do about it now.

Robbie poked Maggie in the arm with his pencil eraser. "Hey! Stop trying to steal our ideas."

Maggie wrinkled her nose at Robbie. "Whatever, Grubby Rubbie!" She waved at me and danced back to her desk.

I sighed and looked at Robbie. "So, why don't we get together after school tomorrow and work on our report?"

Robbie stuck another piece of gum in his mouth. The wad was getting bigger and bigger by the second. It made his tongue turn dark green.

"Can't. I have after school sports," he said, wiping his mouth on his sleeve.

"Hmm, okay so how about *after* dinner tomorrow? I can ask my mom to see if you can come over."

"Cool, I'll let you know."

Mrs. Wayne whistled for attention.

"As part of our Media Communications Unit, our class is taking our annual field trip to the Channel 10 news studio next Monday. For those of you who are auditioning for the *Kidz Konnection* guest host spot, this will be an excellent time to practice in front of the camera, and we'll all get a behind the scenes look at what goes into the news production process." She removed her glasses and rubbed her eyes. "Oh, and don't forget to bring your signed permission slips."

My stomach twisted as I remembered the form I needed Mom or Dad to sign for the audition. Maybe I could swap it out for my field trip slip and then – No. There's no way I could trick them into thinking it was a different form. Dad liked to read all of the fine print anyway.

When the bell rang, Robbie shoved his hoodie into his backpack and took off for the door, yelling for his friends. As I packed up my books, I couldn't decide which was worse: gum-slobbering Robbie as my partner or competing against my best friend in the entire blue and green world.

Wednesday, April 12
Logged on IN A NAT SHELL
(*via Oak Grove Elementary Intranet*) at 5:03 PM:

Hello, friends, family, cousins, pets, everyone out there in the cyber world—

Today in class, we got assigned partners for an out-of-the-box end of the year project. No one got to choose their own partner, so Kailyn, Maggie and I are not together. TEAR!

My partner is Robbie Lovelton. I've never had to work with him before so I hope it goes well. I don't know, though...

That's me In A Nat Shell,

Natalie

TAKE 7

The next day, the doorbell rang as I was helping Mom put away the dishes from dinner. The doorbell ringing meant Robbie was here. I would rather have eaten a whole bowl of Brussels sprouts than have to spent one minute with Robbie. And I hate Brussels sprouts more than peas. But I knew the quicker we started our report, the less time I'd have to see him.

Sydney ran for the door. "I'll get it!"

Mom scooped her up before she left the kitchen. "Natalie, see if it's Robbie before you open the door."

I dragged myself to the hallway and squinted one eye in the peephole in the front door. A GINORMOUS brown eye stared back at me.

Creepy Robbie! I grumbled a quick hello as I let him in.

"Hi, Robbie. Glad you could come over," Mom said from the hallway. "Why don't you two work in the dining room? I cleared off the table for you to work."

I breathed a sigh of relief. No way I was going to let Robbie touch anything in my room. I don't think I would be able to sleep if he –

"Hey!" I grabbed the glass bowl from Robbie's hands and placed it back on the hallway stand. "Don't touch that."

Robbie shrugged. But apparently he didn't get the memo to keep his hands to himself. I flung my arms out to guard as much of Mom's fragile knick-knacks as possible from Robbie's curious hands.

Quick as lightning, he ran ahead of me and dumped his backpack on one of the chairs. A plate of sugar cookies and two glasses of milk sat in the middle.

"Alright! King of the World, right before your very eyes! I *never* get to sit at the head of the table at home." Robbie fist pumped to an invisible crowd. A second later he lunged toward the food, and I watched as a handful of cookies disappeared.

"More like King of the Annoying Ones," I mumbled. "Why don't you get to sit there at home?"

"Where?" Robbie asked looking at me with super chunky cheeks. I pressed my lips together to avoid a laugh from escaping.

"At the head of the table."

He finished chewing before responding. "Oh. That. Because the princess of the house gets her way all the time," he said in a high-pitched mocking-type voice. He poked holes into a napkin with his fingers and put it on as if it were a glove.

"Princess?"

"My older sister."

I stared at Robbie. Nodding my head, I added, "Yeah, boy do I understand. Why don't you try sitting there one day? See what happens?"

"Oh I know what will happen. My sister said she'll send me away if I ever steal her spot," Robbie said, looking at me seriously. He inhaled several cookies faster than I could say "yuck". I highly doubted he chewed them.

I raised my eyebrows, not sure if he was telling the truth. I got out my purple notebook and matching colored pen. Sighing, I said, "Alright, our report. We have to think of a creative presentation that represents fear." I tapped the tip of my pen on my chin.

"Fear. That's easy," Robbie said. "Reminds me of the new video game, *Tower of Trouble*." He snapped his fingers. "I got it! We should have a competition in class. People would definitely be afraid of me. No one can beat the *Tower of Trouble* King." He stood tall and started taking bows.

"Robbie, I'm serious. We can't play video games for our report."

He rolled his eyes. "Whatever Snot-A-lie."

I glared at him. "No name calling, k?"

We sat in silence for the next couple of minutes brainstorming by ourselves.

Tap

Tap

Tap. Tap tap.

Tap tap, tap tap. Tap tap, tap, tap.

I looked up. Robbie was playing the drums with his pencil, his eyes were closed and he bopped his head to some sort of invisible music. How were we ever going to get any work done with Robbie not paying attention?

In the next room, my little sister whined. In a matter of seconds, loud voices rang through the air and disappeared as quickly as they came.

"Holy Cannoli, what was that?" Robbie dropped his pencil and covered his ears.

"Sydney, my little sister. She loves to press all the buttons on the TV remote."

Mom poked her head into the room. "Sorry about the noise, guys. How's the work coming?"

"Terrible," I said. "We have no ideas yet."

Robbie put his hands on his hips. "Don't fear, Robbie is here!" He looked at me and grinned. "Get it? Fear?"

I dropped my head into my hands.

Mom smiled and disappeared into the kitchen. Robbie grabbed four more cookies and stuffed them into his mouth. As he munched on them, crumbs fell all over his paper.

Just as I was about to give up hope that we might get somewhere with our report, Robbie spoke.

"Gwuss whaut? My dad geths to tawk to celebfrities this week," he said through a mouthful.

"Huh?"

Robbie gulped down a big swig of milk. He used his shirtsleeve to wipe his milk mustache.

"My dad is talking to celebrities. During the news."

A celebrity! I'd never met a real celebrity before. Robbie's dad was uber lucky.

"Really? That's so cool. Who?" I asked.

He rattled off a list of names.

"Carrie Moore, Eric Quinton, Allie Marks, Jordan Menter, and some other people I don't know."

"Wait a second," I said. "Did you say Allie Marks?"

"Yup. The one and only. Why?"

I twirled my pen over and over. "Um, no reason."

Robbie stared at me as if he didn't believe me.

"Um. So will she be going anywhere? To sign autographs or something? Where anyone can meet her?" Maybe she'd be at the mall and I *would* actually get to meet her. Then I wouldn't have lied to my friends...*per se*. This might work out after all!

"Nope," Robbie said.

My hopes sank once again.

"My Dad is conducting private interviews with them." He smacked his pencil down and looked me square in the eye. "You have to have a private employee badge. Everyone in the studio is super busy, so only VIP get to meet the celebrities."

I thought about telling him the truth about my lie to meet Allie. Maybe he could somehow talk his dad into helping me out. Even if I didn't get to actually see her up close, but rather from across the room, that would still count, right? I quickly shook the idea from my mind. I definitely couldn't tell Robbie any of this. He would squeal to all of his friends, and the entire fifth grade would know I was a big, fat liar.

No way, José.

Thursday, April 13
Logged on IN A NAT SHELL
(*via Oak Grove Elementary Intranet*) at 7:07 PM:

Howdy bloggers!

Yesterday, Mrs. Wayne announced that we are going to a real, live news studio on Monday. I, for one, cannot WAIT to showcase my skills! If it weren't for *Kidz Konnection*, I would not have a clue on what to do. But, alas, I do. So, fans, stick with me! I'll steer you in the right direction when it comes to being on TV! Here are the top five things you must do before stepping into the spotlight:

1. Check your teeth for any food stuck in them.
2. Spray hair shiner until your hair sparkles in the lights.
3. Do some quick face stretches to loosen up.
   (Warning: If you do this in the mirror, you might laugh!)
4. Do a 30-second dance to shake off the nerves!
5. Smile BIG!

That's me In A Nat Shell,

Natalie

Shared Comments:
Logged on IN A NAT SHELL at 8:34 PM

Hail2KailGal: I totally agree, Nats! Thanks for the advice. Should be exciting to see how it all works. Bring on the spotlight. :)

TAKE 8

Before I made it to my desk Monday morning, I felt a tap on my shoulder. I spun around to find Kailyn directly behind me.

She pressed her finger to her lips for silence and waved for me to follow her to the back of the room.

"Okay, I had to tell you this. A rumor is flying around that you and Robbie-" she paused for a split second "-*like-like* each other."

I gasped so hard I almost started coughing. *Like* each other? Why in the entire blue and green world would someone think that?

"Megan saw Robbie flirting with you," Kailyn said, as if reading my mind.

"What? He was not!" Despite my insistence, I felt my cheeks grow hot.

Kailyn raised an eyebrow. "She said she saw him chewing gum. You know what they say about guys and gum, right?" Her eyes sparkled with excitement. She loved gossip almost as much as I loved *Kidz Konnection*. As the Gossip Queen, she knew everything that happened in school, rumor or not. And she was not afraid to share the news, especially if it meant more attention for her.

Kailyn had the type of stare that nearly got you to admit any secret you ever had stored in your head. I swear, sometimes I thought Kailyn was a snazzy witch with crazy telepathic powers that entranced you and forced you to spill your deepest, darkest secrets.

Maybe she was in the FBI.

I shook my head, dazed from my own thoughts. "No. What do they say?"

"That he wanted to freshen his breath so he could—could *kiss* you!"

I stood there in shock unable to say a word. My jaw locked into place.

Kailyn's face searched mine. "It's okay. I know you don't like him. Megan can make up stories. And listen, I know we're competing against each other, but as best friends and the Divine Girls, I feel it's my duty to—"

The chiming of Mrs. Wayne's morning bell pierced the air.

"Class, y'all to your seats!" she called out in her usual singsong voice.

I waved and darted to my seat. I tried to forget about Kailyn and her secret mind reading skills when Mrs. Wayne whistled for attention.

"Class, I'd like for everyone to get with their partners for your class project. You have twenty minutes to work together, and then we'll be leaving for the studio."

Twenty minutes of report time meant I had twenty minutes to weasel Robbie into thinking of a project idea. I had to be patient and try talking to him.

How hard could it be?

* * * * *

Hard. A gazillion times harder than I thought. Who was I kidding? How did I not see this coming? Of course Robbie would not be easy to work with. As everyone paired up, we slipped to the front near the tank where Shell-E. our class turtle, sat on a rock. She opened an eye and crawled under her makeshift home, apparently miffed that we had disturbed her during her morning nap.

Robbie tossed his notebook onto the small table like it was a Frisbee. It flew across the surface and landed onto the floor with a *THUMP*. I rolled my eyes. Such a boy.

I coughed trying to get Robbie's attention. He clearly was more interested in an ant on the table.

"So, Robbie, how was your weekend?" I asked.

"Why you wanna know?" he said, sitting across from me.

"I dunno, just curious …" I let my voice trail off, unsure of what to say. I didn't want him to think I was nosy.

"Hey. Watch this." He flipped his pencil in the air and tried to catch it behind his back. No luck. It clattered to the floor and rolled over to Mrs. Wayne's desk.

Mrs. Wayne picked it up and frowned in Robbie's direction.

As she walked over, it was hard not to notice her yellow and black outfit. She looked like a big bumblebee. As she got closer, I could have sworn I heard buzzing.

"Mr. Lovelton, I do not believe you are trying out for the juggling act in Cirque du Soleil, so could you please settle down? This is a great opportunity for you and Natalie to work on your report."

"We don't need to do anymore work, Mrs. Wayne. We're mastering our grand plan."

Mrs. Wayne folded her arms. "Oh I see. Already? And what would this master plan be?"

"I can't say just yet. It's a secret." Robbie glanced my way and grinned.

"Well, let's hope it's regarding your report. No more goofing off, young man." As Mrs. Wayne headed back to her desk, I stared at Robbie in disbelief. My head buzzed with frustration.

Robbie noticed me looking at him, but didn't say a word. He pulled out a small packet from his pocket.

"Gum?" he asked, extending his hand out to me.

Part of me thought Kailyn might be on to something. But I was too annoyed to investigate her theory. Too bad I wasn't a bee myself, because if I was, I would have stung Robbie right there and then.

"Are you kidding? We're going to get into trouble! You just lied to Mrs. Wayne," I said.

"About?"

"A plan! We don't have a plan at all."

"I never said that," Robbie said. "I said we're *mastering* one. We'll think of one eventually. And it will be great."

He unraveled four pieces of gum and popped them all into his mouth at once.

I leaned forward in my seat, closer to him. "Okay. So let's brainstorm. What brilliant ideas do you have?"

He leaned away from me. I quickly sat back and noticed for the first time that Megan was staring in my direction. She turned around and giggled.

This was not good. Did it really look like we had a gigantic crush on each other?

"Got it. It's brilliant. What about a big competition of *Ultimate Martian Mix-up*? It's a pretty scary game you know."

I shook my head. "I told you before. Not happening. No video games."

"But you should know I'm really good at –"

"No."

"Oh—I got it! An armpit farting contest!"

"How does that show fear? NO!"

He grabbed the end of his shirt and pulled it up half way. "Actually the sound can be super loud if you –"

"Robbie!" My arm shot out to stop him. We agreed to work in silence for the next ten minutes, but by the motion of his arm I figured Robbie was sketching some sort of alien or beast-like creature in his notebook. Mrs. Wayne called us back together, and the room filled with commotion.

Part of me felt stupid for thinking Robbie would help come up with a useful idea for our project. I could see the big fat ZERO in my horizon. And even worse, my chances to have a killer audition? They were as real as the monsters under my bed.

* * * * *

"Time to pack up and head outside to the buses, y'all!" Mrs. Wayne grabbed her leopard print jacket and whipped it around her shoulders. It looked more like a cape to me. I imagined Mrs. Wayne pretending she was a school super hero, shielding kids from flying chicken nuggets during cafeteria food battles and rescuing others from being shoved into lockers.

As she led the way outside, Kailyn came over to me and looped her arm through mine. Maggie skipped her way up to my other side and did the same.

"I am uber pumped for this field trip," Kailyn said. "I can't believe we will get to meet actual TV news announcers!"

Maggie giggled. "They're called newscasters, Kail."

Kailyn kept going. "I can't wait for the huge stage and bright lights with people running around waiting on you hand and foot, styling your hair, applying makeup, doing your nails—"

"This isn't a spa, you know," I said, giggling, as we climbed the bus steps. We walked toward the back and chose a seat big enough for the three of us.

"Well, maybe they'll choose someone to be part of their nighttime newscast," Kailyn said. Her eyes lit up. "You never know! This—" she paused and stuck her tongue out to the side in thought, "—might be our BIG moment. When we get noticed!"

"I doubt it but you—" Before I could finish my sentence, a string of green slime landed in the middle of Maggie's lap. The three of us screamed at the same time. Maggie flung it to her left on to Kailyn.

"Ew! Get it off me!" Kailyn hurled the goo toward the window, making it stick.

"What *was* that?" Maggie said.

A chorus of laughter rang out behind us.

"Oh, *there* it is." Robbie poked his head over the seat. "Girls, if you wanted my slime ball you should have just asked for it." He peeled the fake goo from the window and barreled into another round of laughter with Zach.

"You are so immature, Robbie," Kailyn said.

"Oh please peas," Robbie whined. "I bet you ten bucks you weren't scared at all. You knew it was fake the entire time."

Kailyn stood, her face red with anger. "I did not! We were having an important conversation until you ruined it."

"Sick. I bet I still have slime guts on me somewhere," Maggie muttered as she checked her clothes.

"Robbie, Kailyn, enough. Please have a seat," Mrs. Wayne called from the front.

We managed to ride the rest of the way with no more Robbie interruptions. Kailyn decided to move up a few seats, claiming she could smell the slime and was getting nauseous. Maggie moved with her for support, but I secretly caught her smelling her clothes, probably hoping it was not her that stank. I stared out the window, hoping we'd get to the studio without any more mega meltdowns.

Would Allie be there? Was it possible that I might actually run into her?

I closed my eyes and tried to picture the moment I'd meet her for the first time:

"Hi Natalie, it's nice to meet you!" Allie said. She hugged me like we were long time best friends reunited. "So you're trying out for the Kidz Konnection *guest host?"*

Despite my nerves, my nose didn't run. "Of course. Wouldn't miss it for the world," I said, beaming.

Allie clapped her hands together. "Aw, that's great! Do you have a partner to interview?"

I shook my head. "Not yet."

"Well that can't happen. How would you like it if I helped you?"

Was she kidding?

"That'd be great!" I exclaimed.

I opened my eyes and grinned from ear to ear. I wondered if Oprah or Ellen felt this way before they met their first celebrity.

As soon as we pulled into the station's parking lot, chatter broke out all over the bus. I felt super important as we rumbled up to the large front entrance. Right above the two revolving glass doors loomed an arching half circle spelling out WRTV-10 COMMUNICATIONS in shiny silver letters.

As we unloaded the bus and passed by the swarm of reporters, I felt almost famous. Some of them turned and glanced in our direction, so I flashed my most dazzling smile at them. I would have bet all of my allowance money that one of them snapped a picture. Maybe the guest host would get to ride in her own limo and walk on a long red carpet! I shook my head. Kailyn's crazy ideas were starting to invade my thoughts.

As we walked inside, I secretly hoped some of her crazy ideas were real.

TAKE 9

The inside reminded me of *Willy Wonka and the Chocolate Factory*. There's a scene in the movie where the end of the hall looks a million miles away, and no matter how much walking you do, you don't get any closer to the door. This hallway was enormous! Pictures of nameless old people with shiny white teeth covered the walls. We walked until I noticed a small waterfall in the middle. Pennies littered the bottom of the fountain.

Oh! A wishing pond. I dug into my purse and searched for a penny. All I found was a quarter. Maybe it would bring me twenty-five times more luck! I closed my eyes and thought about the audition, Allie Marks and the ultimate moment when they would reveal the winner's name…

"All right everyone, the moment we have all been waiting for is finally here! After much consideration, I am pleased to announce the next guest host for Kidz Konnection. *And the winner is –"*

"Excuse me."

Startled, the coin slipped from my fingers and into the pond. I opened my eyes and whirled around. A frowning security guard stood in front of me.

"Are you lost?" he asked.

Looking around, I realized I was alone in the hall. Where was the group?

"I'm with my class. From Oak Grove..."

He motioned for me to follow him. "Come with me."

We walked down to the end of the hallway and turned left. Then another left. And then a third. I felt like a mouse in a never-ending maze.

As we entered the studio, chaos surrounded me. A gazillion people ran around, tossing papers and clipping microphones onto reporters. Others ran up and down a small stage set with a large moon-shaped desk and brightly lit lamps. I recognized it from TV. This was so cool! Me, Natalie Greyson, was in a real, live studio.

As I rejoined my classmates, a man flew by me. And I mean *flew*. He ran around as if his feet were on wheels. (He should think about getting rollerblades.) He wore wrinkled clothes and a large black headset that reminded me of the ones they wore at the Burger Palace when they asked you if you wanted extra whipped cream on your chocolate shake. (The answer is always "Yes, please!")

He barked out orders to the other workers, who in turn, raced off to do what he said. I knew he was The Boss. Lots of people asked him questions, and every time he turned his headset slid down to his neck. At one point he stopped, took a huge breath, and ran his fingers through his hair, which was black with a thick streak of white down the middle. I had to blink my eyes a couple times to make sure he wasn't wearing a skunk on his head. Another man in a nice suit walked over and shook Mrs. Wayne's hand.

"Hi everyone! Great for you to join us." I recognized Robbie's dad, Mr. Lovelton, right away. Earlier this year he had chaperoned a class field trip and was incredibly bossy, ordering for us to always "stay in line" and clucking his tongue when we strayed. After that, I nicknamed him Mr. Meanie-ton. He introduced himself to the class, took a headphone looking-piece out of his ear, and let it dangle on his shoulder. "Come on, we have a bunch of exciting stuff for you to see. By the end of today, you'll be a pro."

Our group followed him past a few cameramen fiddling with the largest cameras I had ever seen. He stopped just short of two steps that led up to a brightly lit stage.

"This is where the newscasters sit to deliver the news several times a day," he said. "Hey Pete, cue the prompter!"

Big, comfy roller chairs were tucked under the long desk. The butterflies in my stomach soared, and the tingles in my hands traveled all the way down my body to my feet. I was where the newscasters sat every day and delivered stories on TV. Maybe Kailyn had the right idea after all. If they let me have a guest spot on the news, and Allie saw it –"

"Uh, please, Zach," said Mr. Lovelton, breaking my daydream and glancing at Robbie's friend. "The equipment here is not to be fooled around with. It is very, very expensive."

I scowled. He was definitely still bossy!

"Ahead of you is what we call the teleprompter," he said stopping in front of a large camera. "You see the words displayed on the screen? As you say them out loud, they will continue to move up. This is more useful than having to constantly look down at your notes, and allows you to connect with your audience."

I rolled my eyes. Who didn't know what a teleprompter was? Any true *Kidz Konnection* fan would. Besides, I had lost count of how many times I had pressed my nose against the window of the Channel 7 News studio on State Street. Being feet away from all of the cameras and newscasters made you feel like you were filming live with them. In fact, sometimes, if you were lucky, you actually made it on camera!

Robbie's dad motioned for Megan to go first alongside Zach. She sat in the chair and banged it against the table as she scooted closer.

"Oops! Sorry. Didn't mean to do that," she said. Zach snickered next to her.

Others soon followed after, but none of them were spectacular. Laura Brown sat down and practically yelled into the small microphone, and Chris Meyer spoke so softly, I wouldn't have been able to make out one word even if I had borrowed Grandpa's hearing aid. Sighing, I sat in a fold-up chair off stage. I couldn't wait for my turn. Unlike my classmates, I had the passion and knowledge to ace this with flying colors. Not even realizing it, my eyelids drooped in boredom. I jerked awake when I finally heard my name being called.

"You want to give it a go?" Mr. Lovelton asked. I nodded as he clipped the tiny microphone to the top of my shirt.

Excitement bubbled up from deep in my stomach as I climbed the steps to the stage. As I fought the urge to scream "I've got this!", I took a deep breath and thought: "think professional." As long as I didn't do anything stupid, the Fake Shakes wouldn't creep their way in. It was time to show everyone how it was *really* done.

Now that I thought about it, I probably should have worn a suit.

"Robbie, why don't you take the seat next to her?" Mr. Lovelton suggested. "For our learning purposes, Natalie, you read the lines on the right teleprompter, and Robbie will take the ones on the left."

I sat straight up in the chair and tried to focus my eyes in front of me. The glare from the lights made me squint to see the teleprompter.

"Pssst!" Robbie whispered. "Read the screen, lima bean!"

I made a face at Robbie, turned back, and took a deep breath.

"Hello." My throat was so dry, it made me sound like a dehydrated frog. Still blinded by the lights, I heard snickering from off to the side. I ignored it, cleared my throat, and focused on the teleprompter. "Good evening. Thank

you for tuning in. We've got breaking news for you today."
I smiled, realizing my voice was back to normal. Shifting
in my seat, I lifted my hand to fix my hair, but ended up
knocking the small microphone piece attached to me. I
gasped as it snapped and fell down my shirt. Looking at
the camera in horror, I tried to shake it out.

"Uh, hold on. Excuse me, I –"

"What are you doing?" Robbie whispered. "Read
your lines!"

"My microphone—it—um, seemed to—" I patted down my
shirt. A loud, grating sound echoed throughout the studio as
the microphone rubbed against the fabric. Next to me, Robbie's hands shot up and covered his ears. I knew if my face got
any redder, it would pop. Swallowing a few times, I forced
myself to stay calm, blinking away any remnants of tearful
humiliation while Robbie took over and read the lines from
both teleprompters. I ducked to the side and quickly wiped
my nose on the back of my arm, hoping no one noticed that
it was running. I knew the Fake Shakes would appear any
minute, and I definitely didn't want them to appear on camera.
I lifted the end of my shirt, and the microphone rolled onto
my lap. I sighed in relief and reattached it to my shirt, but it
was too late. When Robbie finished, I quickly stood and faced
Mr. Lovelton. He frowned, detached the microphone, and
looked it over, probably wondering if I had broke it.

"Not to worry." Robbie's dad smiled at me, but he
looked slightly annoyed. "It takes some getting used to.
It all comes together after practice and more practice." He
glanced over at my classmates. "Who wants to be next?"

A sick feeling crawled its way into my stomach as
I dragged myself off the stage. That had not been what
I wanted to show everyone. I had been "on air" for less than
two minutes, and already I had messed up. If I couldn't
master the practice, how was I supposed to nail the audition *and* be chosen as the next guest host?

As I waited for the others to get a chance on stage, I tried to relax. But my body felt all plugged up with air like the big balloon Mom always bought for my birthday parties. I grabbed a paper cup and filled it with water from a nearby fountain. Just as I had nearly convinced myself it wasn't a big deal, Kailyn took the stage. She sat composed at the desk and looked straight into the camera. The lights reflected off her perfect, shiny hair; her smile genuine. She really did look like a pro.

"This afternoon, the Oak Grove Elementary students visited the WRTV-10 station to learn the ins and outs of news production," she read. "Students toured the studio, met local news anchors, and had the opportunity to present a mock-televised news segment."

She paused and let Jessica Taylor read her part. The back and forth dialogue sounded simple and effortless—the complete opposite of Robbie's and mine.

"That's all for today. I'm Kailyn McAllister. Please have a good evening!" Kailyn cocked her head to one side, smiling and waving at the camera. I rolled my eyes. A bit over the top if you asked me.

But as soon as she stood, our entire class erupted into applause.

"Looks like you all have a natural in the class," Mr. Lovelton said, beaming at Kailyn and patting her on the shoulder. Was Mr. Meanie-ton actually being *nice*?

She skipped off the stage and headed over to Megan and Laura. I overheard her say "Now *that's* how you nail a news segment." She smiled when she noticed me staring at her. I gave her a thumbs up back, but part of me couldn't help but feel bitter. Did she really need to brag?

I crushed the cup in my hand and tossed it into the garbage, trying to shrug off my feelings of self-doubt. Maybe I needed a little more practice, like Mr. Lovelton suggested. When the time came for the actual audition, I would do everything to be prepared and spot on as Kailyn.

But would I be better?

Monday, April 17
Logged on IN A NAT SHELL
(*via Oak Grove Elementary Intranet*) at 8:03 PM:

Blogger friends,

Today, we went to the WRTV-10 studio and got a behind-the-scenes look into news production. It was super cool! The best part was being on stage and pretending to film a live newscast.

The not-so-good part? The small microphone somehow popped off and fell down my shirt, causing me to miss my lines. No worries! This was only P-R-A-C-T-I-C-E. Consider that my C-game. As long as I continue to rehearse, I will get my A-game back and become a master interviewer in time for the big audition!

Some people, (NO NAMES MENTIONED), really should not boast their talent, though. It makes others feel bad. Just saying.

That's me In A Nat Shell,
Natalie

Shared Comments:
Logged on IN A NAT SHELL at 9:10 PM:

MagPie54: It's okay, Nats! Practice makes perfect! I thought Kailyn did great, too!

Logged on IN A NAT SHELL at 9:29 PM:

Hail2KailGal: Thanks, Mags! Natalie, I agree with you except for the last part. Most people in our class aren't meant for the spotlight or TV, but that doesn't mean others should hide their talent.

TAKE 10

As we took out our reading workbooks the next morning, a thought popped into my mind. I had been so busy thinking about doing better than Kailyn that I hadn't figured out who would be my partner. The audition would be here before we knew it! As much as I wished my daydream of Allie asking to be my partner would come true, I knew that would never happen. Or be allowed for that matter.

I quickly tore a piece of paper out of my notebook:

Hi Mag Pie!
Can I interview you for my audition?
Pretty pleaze! :)

I drew two large boxes underneath and labeled one "Yes" and one "No". I added stars and floating streamers and drew smiley faces in balloons. Folding it into a neat square, I scribbled "Private" on the front.

"Natalie!" Maggie said in a rushed whisper.

"What?"

Maggie nodded her head toward the front of the room. Only then did I notice everyone staring at me, including Mrs. Wayne. I crumpled up the note in my hand.

"Natalie, care to share what's so important that you are unable to pay attention?" Mrs Wayne adjusted her glasses on her nose.

"Uh, no, that's okay. Sorry," I mumbled.

"No more notes, Natalie."

I kept my gaze on the front of the class, but the minute Mrs. Wayne turned her back, I flipped the note toward Maggie. The non-athlete in me showed her true colors. The note sailed past Maggie, who clearly wasn't paying attention, and landed near Kailyn.

Kailyn smiled my way. My heart leapt into my throat. That wasn't for her, it was for Maggie!

Kailyn kept her gaze on Mrs. Wayne as she reached her leg out and softly placed her shoe over the note. She then slid it over to her. Pretending she had an itch, she reached down and grabbed it off the floor.

As she slowly opened the note and read it, my breathing slowed and I wondered how she would react. The second she pursed her lips, I knew she realized the note wasn't for her. She quietly folded it back up and shoved it in her folder.

But she didn't look my way.

* * * * *

Kailyn, Maggie, and I had recess before lunch. I was too nervous to move. Or breathe. Had Kailyn already talked Maggie into helping her with her interview so she would win? The both of us trying out for guest host made everything feel supremely weird. This was the first time we ever competed against each other, and deep down I knew I wanted it more than she did.

When Mrs. Wayne dismissed us for recess, I grabbed my light jacket from the back and whirled around just in time to smack right into Kailyn.

"Whoa!" I cried.

Kailyn rubbed her forehead. "Ow!"

"Sorry," I mumbled, pretending my jacket was extra complicated to put on.

Kailyn glanced my way. "Just so you know, you can't interview Maggie."

Who died and made her Queen Kailyn? "If I want to, I can."

"No, you can't," Kailyn said, shoving an arm through her sweater. "And what was with your "No Names Mentioned" in your blog post?"

"What about it?" I said. "And let me guess. *You* are already interviewing Maggie?"

Kailyn put her hands on her hips. "Actually no. Maybe if you had read the entire rules, you would know that your partner has to be a *con-tes-tant*." Maggie skipped over, her ponytail swinging. "And since Maggie isn't trying out, you can't interview her."

Omigosh! I had completely forgotten to go back and check out the rules after the other day at Kailyn's. "It says that?"

Before Kailyn could reply, Mrs. Wayne called everyone to the front, and we walked outside as a group. Several boys, including Robbie, made a beeline for the basketball court. The three of us walked in silence.

"Sorry guys," Maggie finally said, sitting in the grass. "I wish I didn't have ballet practice that day or else I would audition."

"Great. Having no partner means I won't be able to try out, and now it's too late. The audition is this weekend." I stuck the toe of my shoe in the dirt and flipped small chunks into the air. I know I should have gone back to read the rules, and Kailyn being the one to tell me one of the biggest rules was super embarrassing. Part of me couldn't help being annoyed at her.

Maggie gave me a hug and then glanced Kailyn's way. "What about you, Kail? Who's your partner?"

Kailyn sat with a plop, mumbling under her breath.

"Huh?" Maggie said leaning forward.

"Well. The truth is....I don't have one either," Kailyn replied, focusing intently on a blade of grass.

"Way to make me feel stupid for not knowing the rules when you can't try out either." I turned my back to Kailyn and Maggie.

"Well, *I* was going to ask Maggie, but that changed once I read them." She faced the other direction, leaving Maggie stranded in the middle.

A few bees buzzed by and landed on some nearby flowers. The wind blew a lock of my hair in my face, and I batted it away.

"Hey!" Maggie jumped up, breaking the awkward tension. "Then the answer is obvious."

Kailyn and I glanced at her.

"What?" I asked.

"The solution is right in front of us." She motioned to both Kailyn and me.

"You mean, Kailyn" – I pointed to her – "and me? Interview each other?"

Maggie smiled. "Why not? I know it's weird to compete against each other since you're best friends and all, but you guys know everything about one another. You could practically do the interviews in your sleep. Who knows, maybe it will put you at an advantage! Besides, wouldn't it be cool if one of you got it?"

I risked a glance over my shoulder. Kailyn's gaze met mine. Here I was thinking of her as competition, and now we were supposed to partner up? "I don't know. Is it in the *rules*?"

Kailyn glared at me. "Again. You would know if you had read them."

I groaned. I meant it as a joke. Did she really have to keep reminding me about the silly rules?

For a second, I thought I saw a flicker in her eyes similar to when a good idea crossed her mind. But I couldn't tell if it was that, or a reflection from the sun.

"So what do you say, Natalie?" Maggie asked.

Maybe Maggie was right. I should give it a chance and see if it works. And really, did I have any other choice? "She's right. One of us getting the position would be awesome."

Especially if that person was me.

"Exactly. This is so perfect!" Maggie exclaimed.

Kailyn looked skeptical at first but finally caved. "Okay, then we should get to work ASAP. We're going to need to practice every day this week, schedule a shopping trip to the supplies store for note cards, maybe the mall for a new dress, possibly the salon so I can get my nails done –"

"Whoa! You're talking a mile a minute, Kail," I said. Figures she would worry about things other than the interview first.

"We don't have much time, Nats, we need to prepare. Come over tonight, k?"

I got a sinking feeling. "I can't tonight. I promised my mom I'd join them for Family Movie Night."

Kailyn cocked her head. "Natalie, what is more important right now? Watching *The Wizard of Oz* for the millionth time or getting ready for the most important moment in our life?"

I knew she had a point but she also wasn't aware that technically Mom and Dad didn't know I was trying out. Besides, trying to get out of FMN was as difficult as getting a third scoop of ice cream for dessert. Next to impossible.

Kailyn didn't wait for my answer. "Oh, and we should probably aim for around ten questions each."

"Ten?" I repeated.

"Yes, ten. A minute or so per question."

"That seems like a lot."

"I don't think so," Kailyn replied.

"What about eight?"

Maggie giggled. "You guys haven't agreed on one thing yet."

Kailyn half-laughed, half-grunted. "You're right...you know, maybe this is a bad idea."

I eyed her suspiciously, hoping she wasn't using her FBI mind-reading skills on me. I swore I felt the laser beams in my brain uncovering all of my past lies.

"Why? Are you afraid or something?" I asked.

"Afraid? Of what?"

I shrugged. "I dunno. Like maybe I'll nail the audition?"

Kailyn covered her mouth with her hand, but I saw she was trying to hide a smile. "Come on, Natalie. Like the way you did yesterday at the studio?"

My voice caught in my throat, and I clenched my fists at my side. "That was *not* my fault. The microphone must have been loose."

She flipped her hair over her shoulder. "Well, all I'm saying is if we're going to be partners we'll have to practice. And don't take this the wrong way, but practice *a ton*."

"Fine," I said. "I'll come over after school tomorrow instead."

"My house, four pm on the dot. Don't be late," Kailyn said. "And since you can't break free of your movie night, be prepared." She paused. "We may need to pull an all-nighter."

Kailyn liked to say that whenever she could. Her older sister always complained about staying up late to study, so I had a suspicion it made Kailyn feel grown-up to repeat it, as if it was something she did all the time.

Normally, I didn't care that she always demanded to be The Leader, Number One, First in Line, whatever title she wanted at the moment. In fact, I was always her #1 fan. But this time was different. This was something *I* wanted. Something I *had* to have. It felt odd to be partners *and* competing against Kailyn at the same time. My stomach felt queasy as we headed in for lunch. My gut feeling told me it wasn't the omelet I had at breakfast. I crossed my fingers behind my back and silently wished Kailyn wouldn't this time become The Winner.

* * * * *

After school, my stomach still felt as funny as it had earlier. Thinking about my confrontation with Kailyn made me more and more nervous. Between that and Robbie flaking out on our project, I half expected my parents to announce we were moving. That would be icing on the Bad Week cake.

Although, on second thought, if we moved very far away, maybe to Timbuktu, that wouldn't be so bad. None of this drama would follow me. I could even start my own show there.With lights that didn't blind you and microphones that stayed put.

Dad was vacuuming the upstairs hallway, but stopped as he saw me climb the stairs.

"Hey there, how was –" he began.

"It was fine!" I said, and slammed my bedroom door. I half expected him to knock on my door and ask what was wrong, but after a couple of minutes, I knew he wasn't going to. Throwing my backpack on the floor, I plopped into my purple chair and logged on to my blog. I had news to share:

Tuesday, April 18
Logged on IN A NAT SHELL
(*via Oak Grove Elementary Intranet*) at 5:53 PM:

Hello my fellow blog followers!

The time has come to announce that Kailyn and I will be partners for the *Kidz Konnection* audition. The rules state you must interview someone who is also <u>trying out</u>. I know what everyone is thinking: how can you be partners with your best friend?

Here's my answer:

1. Kailyn and I being partners puts us at an advantage. We know each other like a bee knows honey.
2. We could do the interviews in our sleep.
3. If we are honest with each other, we will rock the audition.

I paused and thought about the one thing that I really wanted to happen. I typed:

4. Should it come down to us (crossing my fingers!), I hope it's me that wins!
   Wish us lotz of luck!
   That's me In A Nat Shell,
   Natalie

As soon as I clicked the "Post" button, I knew I shouldn't have posted #4. Of course it was true, and I was technically being honest, but with Kailyn being Miss Competitive, she would definitely be upset. I sighed and placed my cursor over the EDIT button.

Muffled sounds from the hallway diverted my attention away from the screen. I tiptoed over to the door and placed my ear to the door crack. Mom and Dad were whispering but not quietly enough. Bits and pieces floated my way.

"...upset about something...angry...school-related."

"...Sydney...photos...don't know if we...could try..."

I sniffed in annoyance and shook my head. Of course, they would be talking about the twins.

"...possibility to make...Saturday...not old enough... kids...show..."

I pushed my ear harder into the door crack, winced in pain, but strained to hear more. Did they just mention

Kidz Konnection? The floor creaked below my feet, and I froze in case they heard it. The conversation paused, then continued. I let out my breath, unaware that I had been holding it.

"...super tight schedule...no time..."

"...I agree...we should talk..."

No time? Tight schedules? Who else would they be talking about but my brother and sister, who lately, always came first?

"Yes, I agree...later...not what's best..."

"Alright, break the news....sure..."

Break what news? Something I already knew? That the *Kidz Konnection* guest host position wasn't going to happen for me? Clenching my fists at my side, I pulled away and glared at the door as if it were my worst enemy towering in front of me. How could they stand right outside my door and decide without me that the audition was not in my best interest? Shouldn't I be a part of the conversation too? This was the single most important thing in my life, and neither of them could see that. This day was awful! I whirled around and grabbed my backpack. Rummaging around in a stew of pens, broken pencils, and crumbs, I finally found what I was looking for.

The *Kidz Konnection* permission slip I had filled out earlier.

I grabbed a purple feather pen off my desk.

I needed to prove to my parents that this was nothing like anything else that I'd been interested in. This could make me BE someone. And although I couldn't say it out loud, a big part of me knew I couldn't let Kailyn win.

This was the only way.

I *had* to do this.

I lowered the pen onto the paper and scribbled Mom's name in the signature line indicated for a parent. Deep down though, something nagged at me. If there was a Moral Scale, I had slid right off the chart and into the mud.

But what other option did I have? Before I could change my mind, I folded up the slip and shoved it in my backpack, for Mrs. Wayne to deliver to the studio tomorrow.

Shared Comments:

Logged on IN A NAT SHELL at 6:04 PM

Robzilla200007: I can't try out since my dad works for the station. They call it "a conflict of interest" which I guess means no employee's kids can audition. Bummer! It's probably for the best. No one would beat the KINGS OF TV: ROBBIE AND ZACH DOMINATE THE WORLD! I should get a prize for **NOT** tryin' out, cuz now you have a chance to win. You can thank me later.

TAKE II

After school on Wednesday, I dragged myself to the front door of Kailyn's house. I couldn't put a finger on why I was semi-dreading this practice session, but I knew I had to force a smile. The tiny devil on my shoulder was clearly annoying me. Its tiny voice knocked on the door of my mind until I listened. *Maybe you're nervous to compete against your best friend…and lose*, it said with a creepy laugh. I shook my head, wondering why the angel on my other shoulder wasn't coming to my rescue. She should be fired.

Before I reached the door, it flew open, and Kailyn stood there dressed in a dark blue skirt, matching button down jacket, and shiny black flats. Her hair was smoothed back with a headband, and I could have sworn she had mascara on. She looked very grown-up.

"It's 4:03, Natalie Greyson," she said, her hands on her hips.

"Yup, here I am!" I said striking a pose.

"You're late," she said, tapping her wrist. I giggled, thinking she was imitating Mrs. Wayne, until she snapped. "And, it's unprofessional to be late. If you're going to be trying out for a top-notch position on TV, you need to be on time.

People at the TV station will think you are not serious about your job if you don't."

Jeez, three minutes in and Kailyn was acting like I had some horrible illegal habit. I stepped into her front hallway and peeled off my jacket.

"Oh." I forced a smile. "Well, you look very nice. You're all dressed up." I looked down at my own outfit. Jeans, a light purple ¾ sleeve shirt and my favorite sparkly silver slip-ons. Suddenly, I felt weird. Like an elephant in a room full of mice.

Kailyn nodded. "I thought I'd play the part to a T. Get all fancy schmancy now, so at the real interview there are no surprises. As my mom says, it's all 'bout being P & P."

"Huh?" I asked.

"Prepared and professional. I think that's going to be my motto when—I mean –*if* I win." She waved her hand as if her flub was unintentional. As her best friend, though, I saw right through her act. The minute she had said "I win," it felt as if a zombie had plunged its gnarly hand right through my stomach.

"I would have changed, but I didn't have time," I said. At least this was the truth. After school, Mom offered to drop me off on her way to take the twins clothes shopping for their upcoming photo shoot. Lucky for me, she didn't even ask why I wanted to go over to Kailyn's house. Not that I ever needed a reason other than hanging out in the past.

"Let's go to the clubhouse," Kailyn said. "It's all ready."

"Here's our stage," Kailyn said, motioning toward two plastic chairs facing each other. "And this is where the audience will sit." Two bean bags and three pillows, each one occupied by a stuffed animal, faced the chairs.

"We're going to have an audience?" I picked up a chubby, light blue elephant.

"Like I said, we need everything to be as close to the actual thing as possible. Anything unexpected would totally throw us off our game."

Kailyn really seemed to know what she was talking about. Or was she trying to throw *me* off my game? Keep me at C-level like the other day at the studio? I think in some sports they called this intimidation. I pictured Kailyn smearing black lines under her eyes the way football players do. The thought made me giggle.

"What's so funny?" Kailyn asked.

I waved her off. "Nothing, just thinking about something."

Despite not looking convinced, she continued. "Come on, I'll interview you first." She took the elephant from my hands and placed it back in its spot. We both took our seats. Kailyn pulled out a set of note cards from her jacket pocket.

I felt super unprepared. Wasn't this practice? My hands felt clammy, so I shoved them underneath my legs, hoping Kailyn didn't see.

"Hi Natalie, welcome to *Kidz Konnection*!" She turned toward the viewers. "Thank you for the applause. You may all be seated now."

I stared out at the audience of animals. They stared right back.

"So Natalie, let's have everyone get to know you better. How old are you?"

"Um, you already know how old I am," I said, confused.

"I know that!" Kailyn whispered. "But the audience doesn't. Play along!"

"Okay. Um, I am eleven-years-old."

"Great! And when's your birthday?"

"September 10th."

Kailyn tucked a strand of hair behind her ear. "Excellent! So why are you here today?"

I paused, wondering if she was kidding.

"Say *anything*," she hissed. "The audience is *waiting*."

"I'm, I'm here, because, my dream … is to be on TV."

"Your dream is to be on TV? That's fantastic! What would be your dream job on TV?" Kailyn asked. She tapped the set of cards on her knee.

Duh. How obvious. "To be the guest host of *Kidz Konnection*, of course," I replied with a small burst of confidence. I turned toward the "audience" and grinned.

"Time out." Kailyn laid down her cards and clasped her perfectly manicured hands together. "Natalie, we're three days away from the *real* interview. You know you can't say that once we are on, right? If I'm questioning you, it means I'm pretending to already be the guest host. Get it?"

"Okay, then what am I supposed to say?"

Kailyn shrugged. "Since we're pretending right now, you virtually can make up whatever you want. Just don't do that at the real interview. As they say in the movies: 'the truth will set you free'." She floated her arm in the air gracefully, as if for effect.

"Why are you acting weird?"

"I'm not. Just trying to get into superstar mode for the real interview, that's all."

I wasn't so sure about this. "Uh huh."

"Fine, Miss I've-Got-This," Kailyn said. "Why don't you try interviewing me now?"

"Alright, I will."

Kailyn motioned to her seat. "Sit here."

"Why? What's the difference."

Kailyn sighed. "It just does."

So we switched seats. I watched as she dusted imaginary crumbs off hers. She sat cautiously, as if the chair would collapse underneath her, and crossed her legs.

"Ready now?" I asked as if questioning a three-year-old.

"One sec." She smoothed down her hair and ran a finger over her teeth till it actually squeaked clean. "Okay. Now."

I took a deep breath and puffed out in impatience. "So, let's see —"

"Wait!" Kailyn sputtered.

Startled, I nearly jumped out of my chair.

"Where are your notes?" she asked.

"I don't have any."

"Oh," Kailyn said, making a face. "Well. Keep that in mind for the real interview."

I sighed. All this talk about "the real interview" was getting super annoying.

"So, um, Kailyn —"

"You didn't say 'time in'."

"What?"

"You didn't say 'time-in'," Kailyn repeated.

"Why would I say that?"

"Because a minute ago I said time-out to tell you that you can't talk about wanting to be on TV during the real —"

I cut her off before she could say "real interview" one more time. "Alright, alright. Time in." I waited for Kailyn to squeeze another word or two in, but she didn't. "So… welcome to the show, Kailyn. How old are you?"

"I am eleven-years-old."

"And your birthday is?"

Kailyn eyed me warily. "November 24th."

"Great! So why are you here today?"

"Time out again! Natalie, why are you asking the same exact questions as me?"

I shrugged. "Why not?"

"First of all, that's being a copycatter. You don't see Allie and Chloe asking the same questions when interviewing celebrities. Second, you don't want to bore the audience or the judges. They'll expect new questions, not the same as mine." She studied my stunned face and added, "What? I'm just trying to help."

I raised my eyebrows. I wondered if she had forgotten that we were practicing in front of *stuffed animals.*

"Besides, you need to show Allie and Chloe you can be unique," she continued. "Think on your toes."

She didn't know what she was talking about! I *was* unique! She just caught me off guard with her professional jacket and skirt, her pretend studio setup, and her fancy schmancy note cards. I totally would have been prepared had she told me how realistic this would be.

I bit my tongue and decided to ignore her. I would show her my creative side, and you can bet it was a *bazillion* times more creative than hers.

"You know what. I need to take a quick coffee break," I announced.

"Since when do you drink coffee? I don't think talk show hosts take those kind of breaks during a live taping," Kailyn replied.

Know it all.

"Then let's cut to a commercial. I need to use the bathroom." Before Kailyn could say real hosts probably go before the show starts, I climbed down the ladder and went inside the house. Once in the bathroom, I turned on the faucet and splashed water on my face. I practiced my most professional smile in the mirror and smoothed out my outfit before heading back to the "studio", making my entrance as grand as possible. I'd show her.

"Thank you, no applause please. You may all be seated now," I said. I waved toward the "audience."

"They were already seated," Kailyn said grimly. "*I* told them to, remember?"

"Well, maybe they took a break during the commercials, too!"

Kailyn crossed her arms and looked the other way. Every part of this practice session was plain awful. My stomach clenched even more, as if the hand buried inside my stomach was squeezing my guts to a mushy pulp.

"Kailyn McAllister. What's your dream job?" I knew she had already asked me the same question, but too bad! It was my turn to interview, and I was going to do it the way I wanted to.

Kailyn lightly tapped her chin. "Well, my dream job is to eventually be a star."

"And what would be the best part of being a star?"

"I'd get to meet tons of celebrities and have awesome movie roles. Plus, I heard you get your own limo driver and gigantic dressing rooms." Kailyn smiled at the audience.

I leaned over and put my elbow on my knee. "Really? What else does the – "

"Natalie! You're sitting all wrong. It's more professional to cross your legs," Kailyn said. "Here, let me show you."

I picked up the nearest stuffed animal and threw it to the floor.

"That's it! I can't take it anymore! You are being so bossy!"

Kailyn's jaw dropped open. "Well, I wouldn't have to be if you knew what you were doing."

"Oh, like you are perfect?"

"At least *I'm* prepared. You didn't even bring any questions." Kailyn stood, sending her note cards spiraling into the air. "Do you honestly think if it came down to us two you'd actually win?"

I began to say something back, but stopped. How did she know that? Realization struck me like a soccer ball to the chest, knocking the wind out of me. After eavesdropping on Mom and Dad's conversation last night, I had completely forgotten to edit the post! There's no doubt she saw it. I tried to compose myself as best as possible and ignore her comment.

"I didn't know this was a major dress rehearsal, you said it was going to be a practice."

"In case you didn't notice, we *are* practicing."

"No, you are pointing out everything I am doing wrong!" I felt the tears well up.

"Maybe you shouldn't be trying out for host if you're not ready," Kailyn said, crossing her arms.

"Well, maybe we shouldn't have agreed to be partners," I said.

"Well, maybe you shouldn't be here," Kailyn shot back.

"Fine, then maybe we shouldn't be friends!"

Kailyn stared at me for a moment. "If that's how you feel." She went over to the treasure box, opened it, and pulled out a piece of paper. "Then maybe we shouldn't be the Divine Girls!" She ripped the paper in two.

I gasped and pointed. "Was that the—?"

Kailyn tossed the torn papers into the box and slammed it shut. "No more friendship, no more pact, no more Divine Girls."

"Well—fine! Have it your way," I said, turning my back to her.

"Works for me!"

We stayed silent for several minutes. Out of the corner of my eye, I saw Kailyn lean down and pick up the bear I had thrown to the ground. She turned it over as if checking for bruises.

Neither of us budged. Finally, I couldn't take it any longer.

"I think I should go home now," I announced, turning to face her.

Kailyn nodded. "It's obvious we have two different interviewing styles."

"You got that right."

"Guess there's only one thing left to do."

"What's that?" Part of me feared what she might suggest.

"Since it's too late to switch partners, we each should come up with a set of questions for the real interview. I already have mine done, as you know, so you will need to think of some." She looked me over and added, "On your own. We won't practice again."

I thought about this for a second. "Practicing" with Kailyn was much tougher than I thought it would be. I didn't think I could handle another bossy, mean order from her. Nothing could be harder than today's so-called "interview".

"Fine," I said. Kailyn offered her hand, and I shook it.

"Alright then," Kailyn said. "May the best guest host win."

I looked my best friend in the eye. *Oh, don't you worry. I will.*

* * * * *

As soon as I walked into the house after Kailyn's mom dropped me off, I was met with "The Look". Some parents may give a certain facial expression when they think you are talking crazy, but this particular one indicated that I was in T-R-O-U-B-L-E.

I figured it couldn't hurt to play it off like I didn't notice.

"Mom, hey, what's up? How was your day?" I tossed my backpack on the hallway bench and popped my feet out of my shoes. I feigned a yawn and stretched out my arms. "I'm beat. I think I'll head to bed now, actually."

I didn't make it two steps before Mom spoke: "Natalie Louise Greyson. We need to have a talk, young lady."

Oh – the full name. That couldn't be good. I froze in my tracks.

"Look at me."

I slowly pivoted to face Mom. Her eyes blazed. If they could shoot daggers, I'd be pinned against the wall. "I had just gotten home from shopping with the twins when I received an interesting phone call."

My face lit up. "Did we win a million dollars? Oh my gosh, I always wanted something like this to happen! Maggie once watched this show where – "

"Stop. Natalie, the phone call was from the TV station." When I didn't say anything she added, "WRTV-10.

They called regarding the *Kidz Konnection* audition. Ring any bells?"

I managed to squeak out a "yes."

"For some reason, the manager of the show called to inquire about your audition partner you submitted on your form." Mom crossed her arms. "Funny, I don't recall seeing a form. Do you?" The tone of her voice told me she already knew more than she was letting on.

Of course. I remembered previously jotting down Maggie's name, but in my anger the other day, forgot to change it to Kailyn's. No wonder they questioned it, since Maggie wasn't trying out after all, and the rules stated you had to be a contestant. I yawned again. "Mom, I'm super tired and I've had a really bad day. Can we talk about this later?"

"Tough. If you have something you need to tell me, you better do it. *Now*," Mom demanded.

Grabbing my bag and flipping it over my shoulder, I started up the stairs.

"Natalie!"

"*What*?" I yelled back.

Mom put her hands on her hips. "What is going on with you?"

"Nothing!"

"Did you submit that permission slip after we told you no? We didn't sign it," Mom said. Realization lit up her face. "Natalie you *didn't*..."

Somehow it hadn't occurred to me to think of an explanation of how I became a contestant if they found out *before* the audition. All I could think about was *getting* to the audition and proving to them that I could win, and if I could do that, then they would see past all of the other sticky details. Unfortunately, it didn't look like Mom was going to forget this any time soon.

"Okay, yes, I did turn it in," I said. "But I had to."

"Excuse me? Had to what?" Mom asked.

"To show you and Dad that I could do this."

"Natalie! You went behind our backs. And you lied." Mom shook her head. "All you showed us is how dishonest you were."

"But you wouldn't even listen." Tears streamed down my face. "I told you how important this was to me, and you didn't even care!"

Mom closed her eyes. "Natalie. Go to your room. We'll talk about this after dinner."

"But, Mom if you – "

"Natalie. Upstairs."

Tears blurred my vision as I raced up the rest of the stairs and fell on my bed.

Wednesday, April 19th
Logged on IN A NAT SHELL
(*via Oak Grove Elementary Intranet*) at 6:43 PM:

High Alert Blog Announcement: Until further notice, the Divine Girls has been suspended. No further information is available at this time. (However, if you want the juicy details, please see Kailyn McAllister, Miss Pee-Pee, I mean P&P).
    Yeah, yeah, me In A Nat Shell,
Natalie

Shared Comments:
Logged on IN A NAT SHELL at 6:58 PM

MagPie54: What?!?! Is this an April Fool's joke I missed?!

Logged on IN A NAT SHELL at 8:23 PM

Hail2KailGal: FYI: Just so everyone knows:
    1. P&P stands for "prepared and professional".
    2. I will NOT be taking ANY questions at this time.

TAKE 12

An hour later, I was still camped out in my room. My stomach rumbled, reminding me that I hadn't eaten dinner. Maybe I would forfeit dinner forever. If that didn't get Mom and Dad to take me seriously, I didn't know what would.

I cracked open my door and peered through the slit. The soft glow of light reflecting off the downstairs hallway floor told me everyone must be in the kitchen.

I tiptoed over to Mom and Dad's bedroom and quietly closed the door. Picking up the phone next to their bed, I punched in Maggie's number. She picked up on the first ring.

"Mags! It's me, Natalie."

"Hey Nats! What's up?"

"Kailyn is crazy, Mag Pie! I think she has officially lost it. She was so bossy today, acting like she already was guest host or something. And get this—she ripped up our Divine Girls pact. Just ripped it *in half.*"

"Are you kidding me? She didn't!"

"Yes!" I covered the phone and craned my neck toward the door, hoping I hadn't been too loud and attracted any attention from downstairs. When I heard my brother shout something inaudible, I knew the twins were keeping Mom and Dad's attention, and I was in the clear.

"It's officially in two pieces," I said.

"What did you do?" Maggie asked. I could hear her take a swig of a drink.

"Nothing."

"Nats."

"What?" I asked.

"You didn't get angry after that? Clearly you were upset about something or you wouldn't have written that blog post a moment ago."

I sighed. "Alright, you're right. I got a smidgen upset. But wouldn't you have if you were there? I mean, it's your pact, too."

"Well." Maggie paused. "I think I might have stuck some marshmallows up her nose or something."

I covered my mouth and giggled. "Make her eat them afterwards?"

"Ew, no way! I'm not *that* mean," Maggie said.

"Yeah, true," I said flopping onto my back on the bed. "She'd probably turn it into some competition anyway and brag that she could stuff the most marshmallows up her nose."

Maggie groaned. "I don't think that's worth bragging about."

"Definitely wouldn't be as cool as being named guest host of *Kidz Konnection*," I said.

"Not even close!" Maggie exclaimed. "So aside from her ripping up the pact, how did the rest of the practice go?"

I watched the ceiling fan turn in slow circles. "She's just so bossy. And a know it all."

Maggie laughed. "Well, we both already knew that. She loves to compete."

"I guess it doesn't bother me normally but now it's just weird to be her partner and compete against her at the same time."

"Then why did you agree to be her partner?" Maggie asked.

"Mags, it was your idea."

"Right, but you didn't have to take my idea. You guys aren't the only two trying out."

I groaned and sat up. "I didn't have a choice. It was too late to find anyone else." But I couldn't help wondering if maybe deep down I was secretly glad to be Kailyn's partner and didn't even know it. Getting to be the guest host on TV instead of her would probably drive her crazy with jealousy.

"Well, honestly, I'm glad you guys are partners," Maggie said. "Blowing away the competition should be a piece of cake."

"Nothing is easy once she gets bossy," I muttered.

"She's just being Kailyn," Maggie said.

"No, she was acting really weird, too."

"Hmm. Well, you know how she gets when she has a bad hair day or her glitter nail polish doesn't match her outfit," Maggie said.

"I guess," I said. Talking to Maggie made me feel a teensy bit better. Could it really be that maybe Kailyn had a bad day just like I had? Maybe her parents had just scolded her for something right before I came over, and she took it out on me.

As soon as I heard the rumble of footsteps and the clatter of plates, I knew it was nearing the twins' bath time. I wondered if Mom or Dad had peeked in on me yet, only to realize I wasn't in my room. I should have stuffed my pillows under my comforter to make it look like I was sleeping, just in case.

"Gotta go, Mag Pie. The twins are on the prowl."

* * * * *

Dad came up ten minutes later. Still lying on my bed, I glanced at him through strands of disheveled hair as he walked toward my dresser. He picked up the picture of my friends and me at the bowling alley, the same one I had looked at before.

"You know, I remember this. You had such an awesome time. You talked about it for days." He came over to the bed and sat next to me. Leaning over, he handed me the frame. "So what changed?"

"What do you mean?"

"Exactly what I asked. What changed since then? Every time you've been interested in something, you've put your whole heart into it, which I'm so proud of. But you've never gone as far as lying and disobeying us."

I mulled that over for a minute. But all I could come up with was that nothing else was like this. Nothing else involved the *Kidz Konnection.*

"I really, really want this," I said finally. "You even admitted the other day that I'm obsessed!"

"Natalie, it's okay to want something badly. I'm extremely happy you found something that makes you passionate and excited and so driven." Dad's smile transformed into a firm line. "But *nothing* should ever make you lie and go against our wishes."

"So am I in trouble?"

Dad looked at me sternly. "Well you're definitely grounded."

That didn't sound too bad.

"For two weeks."

I groaned. That did. "So what about the audition?"

"Your Mom and I thought about this. In most cases, I would say no, and that would be the final decision. However…"

My heart leaped in my chest, and I took a deep breath.

"You can audition—"

I jumped up on the bed, my stuffed animals flying left and right. "Oh Dad, thank you, thank you –"

"—under one condition."

I froze, my arms shoulder high, poised for a hug. "Condition? What sort of condition?"

Dad stood. "You need to take responsibility for your actions, good or bad. So you will need to call the station yourself and let them know what you did."

I looked at Dad, horrified. "But – but Dad – they will say no! They will disqualify me! Cut me loose! Tell me sayonara! Adios! Auf Wiedersehen!"

Dad shrugged. "If they do, then so be it. But either way, you need to call them and be honest. If you are going to even *attempt* to audition, and they allow you to, you will do it the right way." He turned and left without another word.

Five minutes later, I was still staring at the door as if I could see through it and into the hall. I couldn't believe my bad luck. And I thought it had turned around, that maybe Mom and Dad finally realized why I took the risk I did. After all, it was just a signature right? They had to see how much this meant to me. But instead, they were practically dangling it over my head like a fish on a hook, just slightly out of my reach. Now I had to call the station? There's *no way* they would allow me to audition. It was like setting your own mousetrap. And I was caught trying to steal the cheese.

* * * * *

The next day I thought about what Maggie had said last night on the phone. Maybe she was right. It wasn't a surprise that Kailyn got so competitive. Normally it didn't bug me.

But the more I thought about it, the more I knew this time was different because I wanted it more than the world.

"Who wants to go on the swings?" Kailyn asked while on our way to recess.

Maggie shrugged. "I will, but no twisting me around. I got so dizzy last time I nearly threw up."

Kailyn laughed like it was the funniest thing in the world. "Oh Mags, you're hilarious."

"I'll swing too, Kailyn," I said.

I wasn't sure, but I thought I heard Kailyn mumble. "Kail?"

"Okay!" she exclaimed.

I flinched in surprise. "Sorry! I didn't hear you."

"My mom says listening is a skill."

I frowned. "I was listening."

"Hey," Maggie said. "No fighting, k?"

"Say that to Miss Bossy Brains." I jerked my thumb in Kailyn's direction. "In case you forgot: she's the one who ripped up the Divine Girls pact."

Maggie froze in front of the swings, holding a marshmallow just below her lips. "Kailyn, seriously, why did you rip up our pact?"

Kailyn glared at us both. "Miss Uber Unprepared here said she thought we shouldn't be friends. And to be honest, I don't think she's ready to be on TV, if you ask me." She crossed her arms and stuck her nose in the air. "And whatever happened to "meeting" Allie? I bet you never were."

"I was too! But—she got busy. She's a celebrity you know. She has very important things to do. VIP," I said, thinking back to what Robbie said. I felt bad for lying but Kailyn probably knew all along that I didn't have any chance of meeting Allie. I wasn't about to give her the satisfaction of knowing that. Not while we were partners.

"Exactly! Why would she want to help out a stranger for the audition? Besides, if she helped you, she would need to help everyone. It'd be only fair," Kailyn said.

"At least she would have been nice. Maybe if someone had warned me about you being a drill sergeant, I would have been more prepared yesterday," I shot back. If I didn't get the guest talk show host position, maybe I would become a judge so I could bang my gavel as loudly as possible and send Kailyn straight to jail for being a mean, bossy friend.

"I shouldn't have to tell you that!" Kailyn said. Her ears turned red, the way they always did whenever she got super mad.

"A *best friend* would."

"*I* think a real best friend would be happy I'm trying out too, and not be jealous."

"Well, a *real* best friend – "

Maggie waved her hands in front of us. "Wait, wait! Stop fighting! Don't make me use a pirouette just to separate you both."

I smiled a little. Maggie always tried to make her ballet moves sound more karate-like than graceful.

Maggie sighed. "What happened? You guys were okay being partners a couple days ago."

I scowled. "It's kind of hard to be partners with someone when she thinks she's Miss Great."

"I can't help it if I'm used to the spotlight," Kailyn said. I snorted.

"Practice makes perfect. I'm sure by the time the audition arrives, *both* of you will be super prepared!" Maggie said.

But Kailyn ignored her and stared at me. "You just wait. In two days, we'll see who the judges like better."

My stomach twisted in a weird way. Not quite a butterfly excitement feeling either. After last night, I knew I needed to rethink my approach and come up with new questions to ask the Talk Show Host Encyclopedia Queen. Oops, Kailyn.

Back in the classroom, I jotted down my ideas, but I didn't have many. All I could think about was my fight with Kailyn. Apparently, I was a space cadet and didn't hear Mrs. Wayne instruct us to pair up with our partners.

"What are you doing? Writing gossipy notes?" Robbie asked me.

"None of your beeswax." I shoved the piece of paper in my glitter notebook and scooted my desk around so it faced his.

"Time to work on our report. Let's see what you've got." He slouched into his seat and rested a dirty shoe on top of my desk.

"We haven't decided what we're going to do yet," I said. I used the end of my pencil to lift his shoe, but it snapped in two. Robbie snickered and shook his head.

"Alright," I said, ignoring his laughter and picking out a new pencil from my case, "let's go over my old ideas. We should think of a few more and pick one today, so we can start working on it at home. I'll do my half, you do yours." I grabbed my notebook and flipped it open. My list of inter-view questions flew out and glided to a stop near the back of Robbie's desk. I leaned down to grab it, but Robbie was too fast. He stomped his dirty shoe on the paper before picking it up. A brownish-green mark stained the back.

"Robbie! Please give that back," I said, trying to swipe it out of his hand.

"Not so fast, Nut-a-lie." He glanced at the questions. "Ah-ha!"

I raised my eyebrow. "What are you "ah-ha-ing' about?"

Robbie rubbed his chin in slow motion. "Interesting, veeeeeery interesting."

I kept my hand held out. "Give it to me!"

"So...I see the problem," Robbie said.

I leaned forward and snatched the sheet out of his hands. "There IS no problem."

"So you think," he said.

"Okay smarty-pants. Tell me the so-called problem," I snapped.

Robbie leaned in. "Kailyn decided to be your partner so she could look better."

I sat there with a stunned look on my face. How much did Robbie know? Had he heard us fighting earlier?

"She knows by you two being partners, she has a better chance of winning."

"What's that supposed to mean?" I asked, shifting in my chair.

Robbie played with a piece of grass stuck to the desk. "Come on, Natalie. We all know you're not as experienced as Kailyn in front of people."

"Not true!" I snapped. "Not that it's any of your business, but we practiced, and it went very well." Somehow I felt like he saw right through my lying, making me feel even worse.

"Well, alright," Robbie said blowing the blade into the air. "I guess the audition can't go as bad as our field trip the other day, huh?"

I glared at him. First Kailyn, now Robbie? "You don't know what you're talking about. So stay out of it." I couldn't believe how this day was turning out. A fight with my best friend, my favorite pencil breaks, and now my partner was being the biggest turd.

The rest of the school day was as much fun as going to the dentist. By the time I climbed on the bus, I felt as bad as if I had a huge cavity. And no Novocain in sight.

* * * * *

My cheeks burned with anger as I stormed through the house. Tossing off my shoes, I raced up the stairs two at a time to my bedroom. I decided to make a list of all the things I needed to keep my mind off of:

Thursday, April 20th
Logged on IN A NAT SHELL
(*via Oak Grove Elementary Intranet*) at 5:03 PM:

To anyone reading this out there, I'll keep this post short—
Things I Am Soooo Over

1. Mean best friends
2. Gross Robbie
3. The twins and their photo shoot

I hesitated and finally typed:

4. The *Kidz Konnection* audition! :(
T.M.I.A.N.S.,

Natalie

Other dislikes would have made the list, like the Brussels sprouts Mom always made or slimy noodles that stuck together, but as of right now, they didn't seem as dire. Bits and pieces of last night's practice session crossed my mind. What made Kailyn so bossy? For someone who barely knew the show, it was odd for her to act like she wanted it so much. And how could she *think* of ripping up the Divine Girls pact? I grabbed some paper off my desk and scrunched it into a ball. With all of my might, I flung the paper wad toward the *Kidz Konnection* poster hanging on my wall. It soared way, way left. Clearly, I was not meant for softball.

And now, who knew if I was even meant for TV?

After my talk with Dad, he gave me the name and number of the employee from the studio who had called the house.

If I had a dandelion in front of me, I would have plucked it and made a wish. A wish that I didn't have to do this. On second thought, I would eat smelly Brussels sprouts or slimy, stuck-together-nasty noodles if it got me out of this pickle.

But that was not the case.

I sat on the edge of the couch with the phone and heard the dial tone ring on the other end. My leg jiggled as I waited. In the background, the TV was on, but the sound was set low. Mom sat next to me and glanced at the screen every now and then as she flipped through paperwork of some sort. The glasses on her nose kept slipping down, but she pushed them back into place just before they fell.

"WRTV-10 Communications. How may I direct your call?"

I cleared my throat. "Um, hi, my name is Natalie. Natalie Greyson."

"Which department are you looking for?"

"Uhh…the TV one?" I had the number and name of the person to contact, but no idea which department he was in.

The lady on the other end seemed impatient. "Can you be more specific, miss?"

I glanced at the slip of paper. "I'm actually looking for a Louis Tanner. He called my—"

"Please hold." The line clicked silent, and for a second I thought she had hung up on me. A few minutes went by. I glanced over at Mom. She looked up at me and winked.

"This is Louis. May I ask who is calling?"

I cleared my throat once more, hoping it didn't disturb him. "Uh, yes, hi. My name is Natalie. You called my house."

"Excuse me?" Louis asked.

I crumpled the paper in my hand. Come on, Natalie, of course he doesn't know you. He's probably called a million houses by now. "Oh uh, sorry. I'm signed up to audition for the *Kidz Konnection* audition, and I was calling to—"

"Last name, please?" Louis said, interrupting.

"Greyson."

The sounds of papers shuffling and the clicking of a keyboard drifted through the phone. "Ah yes. Natalie Greyson. Just received your information today. Oak Grove Elementary. How can I help you, Natalie?

Despite me not being in front of a crowd, I could sense my Fake Shakes coming through. It probably wasn't everyday Louis received a phone call about someone who lied to get their way into the audition. If I felt bad before, it was ten times worse now.

"I'm signed up for the *Kidz Konnection* audition," I finally stammered.

"Yes, you already mentioned that," Louis said. "I also see in my notes that we called you regarding a Maggie Castlebury as your partner, but she is not in our records as auditioning."

"Actually, I have a new partner, but the reason–"

"Name?"

"Excuse me? Oh, uh, sorry, I thought I gave that to you already, Natalie…"

"No, the name of your new partner," Louis said.

"Right! Sorry! Kailyn McAllister."

There was more clicking on the other end, followed by some murmurs. "Yes, we have her in the system. It appears she has already updated her file with you as her partner so we will go ahead and process this information. Thank you for returning our phone call."

"Oh, well, wait!" I said, afraid he might hang up.

"Yes?"

I took a deep breath. "I actually need to tell you something. To confess something." Mom looked up from her papers and nodded once my way.

"I'm sorry?" Louis said.

Like ripping off a Band-Aid, I did it fast. "I-forged-my-parent's-signature-on-the-permission-slip." My heart was racing. "I'm so sorry."

Louis was quiet for a second. "I see." He paused. "Are you calling to remove yourself from the audition list then?"

"I don't want to, but you see, my parents would only allow me to audition if I informed the station of what I did." I fought back the tears that threatened to arrive. Any moment now, Louis would tell me how awful I was and just how grateful *he* was to know that a liar would not be auditioning for one of his station's shows.

Louis sighed, and I swear I could hear him scratch his head, but my ears were probably playing tricks on me. "Well, Natalie, I appreciate your honesty. I can imagine this was not an easy thing for you to do."

"No sir, it wasn't. I'm sorry," I said.

I could picture Louis rubbing his eyes in exhaustion. "However, since the audition process has not yet begun, and the deadline is tomorrow, if you can submit an updated form with an authentic parent signature, we'll replace the current copy in our files."

Either my heart stopped or my breathing did, but regardless, I could barely move. "Really? You mean I can still audition? I'm not fired?"

Louis half-chuckled. "Well, no. Firing is not my department, it's actually over at – uh well, I digress. Please make sure to include your new partner's name on the form as well."

I motioned to Mom for her pen and quickly wrote down Louis's email address. After apologizing and thanking him one more time, we said our good-byes.

I put down the phone and glanced at Mom.

"Well. From the looks of it, it appears you just got lucky, Natalie," she said. "Just remember, second chances don't come very often."

I nodded vigorously and rubbed my acorn necklace. I couldn't agree with her more.

* * * * *

Later that night, I lay in bed, too excited to sleep. I stared at the neon green numbers glowing from my nightstand alarm clock. As I watched them take what felt like infinite amount of time to change, my mind traveled back to Kailyn and how she was preparing for the Big Day. Was she keeping the questions she had asked me before? Or was she at this very millisecond thinking of new ones? What if they were perfect, exactly what the judges were looking for, and they topped mine? Or worse, what if I didn't know the answers and ended up looking silly? My head spun as I envisioned sweat dripping down my face, hands shaking as I sat with my mouth open trying to force words out that didn't want to. What if an air burp escaped?

I closed my eyes and took three deep breaths. Then I counted to fifty and told myself to repeat. Eventually, all my deep breathing exercises must have lulled me to sleep. The next thing I knew my alarm was going off.

At breakfast, I poured a bowl of cereal and watched as Mom fussed over getting the twins ready for school. Dad sipped his coffee while reading the sports section of the newspaper.

"Woo!" he wailed out of nowhere.

I practically choked on my cereal.

"Yea, White Sox! That'a boys!" Dad said. He folded up his paper, took one last giant swig of his coffee and placed his mug into the sink.

"Hi ho, hi ho, off to work I go," Dad said in a sing-song voice.

Mom blew him a kiss, and the twins waved. Right before he left the kitchen, Mom hollered at him. "Don't forget to charge the good camera. We'll need some nice pictures of our own tomorrow."

I paused, my spoon in mid-air. "Uh, please no pictures tomorrow. I'll be nervous enough as it is!"

Mom and Dad stared at me.

"Oh sweetheart, I meant for the photo shoot," Mom said.

"But we'll try our very best to be there by the time they announce the guest host," Dad said trying to look optimistic.

"Wait a second – you guys made me call the studio, admit something completely embarrassing, and you won't even be there to see me audition?" I asked.

"Of course we want to be there, but you know we already committed to the photo shoot." Mom grabbed the twin's jackets from the hallway.

I couldn't believe what I was hearing. Suddenly, it tasted like I was chewing lemon-flavored flakes. I grabbed a napkin and spit out my food.

I may have gotten lucky by getting to still audition. But part of me wondered if I was lucky enough to overcome my nerves, outshine Kailyn *and* knock the socks off of the judges.

And do all of that without my family there.

* * * * *

Audition Day.

I jumped out of bed before my alarm went off. Today was The Big Day! For my special interview, I chose to wear my sparkly purple shirt, dark blue jean skirt cut off at the knees, and light purple bracelets. Saving the best for last, I slipped my acorn necklace on. It glinted in the mirror. A future guest host image stared back at me. After I tried out a few different smiles and settled on one, I raced around the house trying to get ready and checked to make sure everyone was on time. Dad finally had to tell me to calm down when I ran into Chase and spilled cereal all over the kitchen floor.

"Alright, you. Save your energy for the stage," he said. "Good luck! Hopefully we'll see you there." He gave me a quick hug and kiss, and left with the twins.

From the moment we left our garage until we arrived at the studio, the butterflies in my stomach grew until they were gigantic and fluttering uncontrollably. I stuffed a wad of tissues into my pocket–in case my nose decided to work against me later.

"You ready?" Mom asked, turning around to look at me.

"I was born ready!" I said pumping my fist into the air.

"Knock 'em dead!" She gave me a quick kiss, and I jumped out of the car.

I appreciated the best wishes from Mom and Dad, and crossed my fingers they would be able to make it.

Once inside the building, everywhere I looked the place was jam-packed with both familiar faces and others I didn't know. Behind me, moms were running through interview lines with their kids, fixing ties, and restyling hair. I felt a twinge of sadness. It would have been nice to have Mom or Dad here to help calm my nerves. While some kids appeared comfortable and at ease, others hopped from one foot to the next in anticipation. Next to them, toddlers whined about being hungry or having to use the bathroom. A few dads, some with very little hair, stood in the corner together checking their phones and talking about baseball. I scanned the crowd for Kailyn but didn't see her anywhere.

Several lines of participants jutted out from a table in the hallway. Signs indicating the first letters of everyone's last name were pinned to the tablecloth. I got in the line labeled F – J.

"Name?" the lady behind the table asked.

"Natalie Greyson."

She made a check on her list and handed me a bright, multi-colored folder with the *Kidz Konnection* logo inscribed on the front. "Inside, you'll find your name tag and what time you are scheduled to interview."

My heart soared. A special folder made for the show contestants! I opened it and glanced at the interview sheet. There were forty names listed, most of them I recognized from other classes. The unfamiliar ones were probably from other local schools. Then I saw Kailyn's name. She was Spot 19. I was Spot 20. A 5-minute break separated each partner's interview.

I wondered if Kailyn was mad she wasn't Spot 1, or if she was just happy she was going before me. I sighed in relief. At least I'd have some time to prepare myself during the break. This way I had a moment to check my teeth, wipe my nose, or use the bathroom before I interviewed her.

Soon, adults with badges started coming around and asking us to find our seats. A heat wave began at the top of my head and worked its way down. I felt a tingling sensation in my hands and feet as we all headed toward the main stage. I wriggled in excitement. It was starting!

Signs pointed to a different part of the studio than where we went for our field trip. As soon as I entered the room, I gasped. Right there in front of me was the *Kidz Konnection* stage. From the way the chairs were set, to the bright overhead lights, to the multi-colored carpet—everything told me I was at my favorite show's home. I followed the others to the seats reserved for those auditioning. The chairs were dark maroon and squishy. They reminded me of movie theatre seats, only cleaner. Much cleaner.

"Laura Brown, you're up," a lady said.

I squirmed as she took a seat on stage across from her best friend, Kristen Jacobs. Maybe I wasn't the only one interviewing her best friend. With this week's craziness, I hadn't thought to see who others were partnering with. Laura was quieter than on the field trip, but she said "um" so many times, I thought she had them written in her notes. When she was done, the crowd gave her a big round of applause anyway.

I clapped too. It must have been super hard for Laura to go first. I suddenly felt incredibly lucky to get a later spot. Jordan Ricefield and Zach Walsh had Spots 3 and 4. Jordan sneezed so many times, he had to leave and grab a big box of tissues. I think he does that when he gets nervous. Or maybe he was allergic to something on stage.

The interviews lasted only a few minutes. I was surprised to hear so many of the kids gushing about how much they enjoyed the show and how badly they wanted to be the guest host. I thought about how Kailyn had said we needed to pretend to *already* be the host. I glanced around and spotted her in the last row. I raised my hand to wave but realized I was still miffed, so I lowered my arm and scratched my head like I meant to the entire time. Before I knew it, we were up to Carrie Wilson and Monica Gilbert, who were right before Kailyn and me. This was my cue to leave and meet in the hall.

Kailyn was already there, pacing back and forth. She reviewed her note cards and mouthed words to herself.

As soon as she noticed me, her face went as white as a ghost.

"Hey Kailyn."

"Hey."

Despite our fight, a huge smile escaped onto my face. "We're minutes away from being on stage auditioning for this great show. Aren't you so excited?"

Kailyn nodded. How could she stay so calm?

"Are those all of your questions?" I asked, trying to peer over her shoulder.

She hugged her note cards close to her. "We don't want to sound too rehearsed. We want to sound natural."

An adult with a small notepad rushed over to us. "Kailyn McAllister?"

Kailyn's hand shot into the air.

"And your partner -- "

"Right here," I interrupted. I leaned over and extended my hand. "Natalie Greyson."

The lady raised one eyebrow. She made a quick note and rushed back into the auditorium. I pulled back, embarrassed to have my handshake request ignored. But I didn't have time to think too much about it. Our names were called, and the audience clapped.

Kailyn's hands shook at her sides, and she took some deep breaths. "Here we go."

TAKE 14

As we climbed the stage steps, the black Mary Jane shoes I had picked out for Christmas clicked their way across the stage and echoed throughout the studio. I would bet all of my allowance money that even the people sitting in the very back heard them. I half expected Kailyn to turn around and tell me to be quiet, that loud shoes were unprofessional, but thankfully she didn't.

The stage was set up similar to the way Kailyn had designed it back in our clubhouse. Aside from no stuffed animals, there were two large microphones by each armchair, and the judge's table was situated off to the left. My heart raced as soon as I spotted Allie Marks and Chloe James sitting behind it, holding huge pink and purple feathery pens over sheets of paper. They looked serious, but smiled when I glanced their way.

I barely had time to get comfortable before Kailyn launched into her first question.

"Welcome," Kailyn said, her voice booming. She swallowed hard and backed further away from the microphone.

"Thanks." I crossed my legs as professionally as possible.

"Please introduce yourself to everyone."

"My name is Natalie Greyson."

"Great! So tell us a little bit about yourself." Kailyn stared straight at me.

Part of me wanted to laugh at my nerves earlier. I was such a worrywart! This was going to be fun. Better not mention I want to be host, like Kailyn had coached me. Of course that wouldn't sound natural. And we would set ourselves apart from the competition. Everyone, look out! Here we come!

"I'm eleven-years-old and love to write. I have my own blog and hope to become a full time author one day," I said.

Kailyn nodded, licking her lips in thought. "Uh huh. What else?"

"Let's see. I'm such a klutz—I'm always tripping over something no matter where I am - and I can be super corny sometimes, but the cornier the better, right? My mom and dad say I'm actually really funny." I smiled, but on the inside I wanted to scream: *Stop rambling, dummy!*

Kailyn giggled, though it didn't sound like her normal laugh. "Totally true! I've known you my whole life, and you're the Queen of Klutziness." She paused. "Remember when you offered to carry in our teacher's surprise birthday cake and ended up dropping it on the floor? What a mess!"

Soft chuckles floated through the audience.

Huh? That never happened. Why would she say that?

Sweat began to form underneath me on the chair. I uncrossed my legs, took a deep breath, and leaned in close, but a loud sound reverberated through my microphone with a piercing *EEEEEEEEEE!* Several audience members covered their ears. Noooo! This was not happening again! Not during the real interview! My hands shook, and I felt my nose run. I tried to move the microphone back. The room felt like it was a hundred degrees. My eyes burned, tearing from the bright stage lights. Great. The judges are going to think I'm crying! Blubbery, just the kind of quality they are looking for in a host.

Kailyn flipped to her next note card. "Do you think in order for someone to be on TV, they need to be prepared and professional?"

Where was she going with this? "Yes…" I said. "But you should also have fun. It's a kid's show after all." I looked out at the audience, but couldn't make out any familiar faces. I smoothed a lock of hair, now slicked with sweat, out of my eyes.

"Have you ever been on a real studio stage before?" Kailyn questioned.

I nodded my head. "Only once before today. For a school field trip."

"And how did it go? Would you say you were professional?"

I scrunched my eyebrows. "Well, I did the best I could. It was first time jitters, I guess."

"Tell us about the microphone mishap during the field trip," Kailyn said.

My breath caught in my throat as I struggled to find the right words. "It snapped off my shirt."

"Of course, it could happen to anyone. So you'd agree it takes a lot of practice before someone can be on TV, right? And it's harder than it looks?" Kailyn asked, smiling like she was trying to sell me a used dirty toothbrush. What a brat!

I gritted my teeth as I realized what my best friend was doing.

"I don't think the microphone was attached properly, that's all," I said with a wave of my hand, trying to play it off like it happened all the time.

Kailyn ignored me. "I've been watching *Kidz Konnection* since it began, and it's become one of my *favorite* shows." She stared beyond me at Allie and Chloe as if I wasn't there and it was solely her and the judges.

My mouth fell open so wide I thought it would hit the floor. Her favorite show?

"I've realized after seeing almost *every episode* that it takes practice and skill to become a great host like Allie and Chloe," she stopped and cleared her throat, "and it would be an honor to be one alongside them. With my singing and talent show experience, I believe I have what it takes."

I bit my lip so hard I thought it might bleed. Before I knew what was happening, the words traveled up my throat like boiling hot lava. I tried to shove them back down, but they forced their way out. I launched out of my seat and glared at Kailyn.

"That's not true! It's not your favorite show! You barely knew the name of it until the announcement!" My arms and legs felt like they were on fire, and my whole body turned to stone when I realized what I had done. I plopped back down, praying I didn't just make a complete fool out of myself. If I had, becoming guest host would now be as easy as winning the lottery.

Allie and Chloe scribbled notes on their paper. Kailyn ended her interview with a quick "Thanks for interviewing with me!" and flounced off the stage. The audience applauded as we exited. Hot tears sprang from my eyes. What if Allie and Chloe agreed with her and made her the new guest host?

The slimy worms inside were attacking the butterflies I had from this morning. My head buzzed uncontrollably. I couldn't believe she had told me what *not* to say during an audition just so she could win.

Robbie was right. Her questions made me look like an unprofessional rookie. How dare she do that to me? Now I only had a few minutes until it was my turn to interview her, leaving no time to re-do my own questions.

A few photographers from our local newspaper snapped their cameras in our direction. Kailyn paused, freezing into a few model poses. Throwing my hands up, I darted past them and down the hall.

I was doomed. The Humiliation Police might as well blow their whistle and come and drag me away before it got any worse. My biggest nightmare had come true. How did this day just backfire on me?

As I sailed out of the door, so did my last bit of hope.

* * * * *

I made a beeline to the bathroom. When I was alone in the stall, I grabbed a bunch of toilet paper and wiped away my tears. With my nose runny and my eyes all puffy, I was a mess. How could Kailyn embarrass me in front of everyone, especially the judges? I balled up my soggy toilet paper and flushed it down the toilet. I waved at the swirling water. "Good bye, dream."

I took out my note cards. I barely had looked at them all day, but it didn't matter. I could recite every question by heart, even what color note card it was on. As I flipped through my cards, the bathroom door swung open, its creaking hinges echoing across the marble floor.

"I can't believe what just happened. How humiliating," said a girl.

Another girl piped up. "I know! That was awful."

I felt the hot tears spring back into my eyes. Of course everyone was talking about my horrible moment on stage. I could see the newspaper headline now:

TOP STORY
ELEVEN-YEAR-OLD OAK GROVE ELEMENTARY
STUDENT LOSES COVETED GUEST HOST POSITION
TO TALENTED BEST FRIEND

"But it's not too late," said the first girl. "This is why we have both interview each other. She can come back and rock her interview."

"Totally! It takes guts to pick yourself up after that mess," said her friend.

I inched closer to the stall door, straining to hear more. The tone of their voices sounded familiar. I heard the girls wash and dry their hands. "Time to shine!" one said. The other giggled. My jaw dropped, and the excitement I felt every Monday afternoon seeped into my bones. I *knew* that phrase. Allie and Chloe said it before every *Kidz Konnection* episode!

I pressed my hands on the door and peeked through the slit, clamping my mouth shut to keep from crying out. It WAS Allie and Chloe! As soon as they left and the door banged shut, I unlocked the stall door. My heart raced. I had just been feet away from my two favorite celebrities! At the sink, I splashed some cold water on my face and stared at my reflection in the mirror.

"I'll prove to the judges I can do this. I'm Natalie Greyson!" I looked in the mirror and rubbed my acorn necklace. "Time to shine!

As I left the bathroom, I smacked right into somebody leaving the boy's room.

"Whoa! Look where you're going," said Robbie.

I mumbled a quick sorry, turned, and walked away.

"Hey, you ready for your interview?" he called after me.

I paused and turned around. "Yes," I said, thinking about Allie and Chloe. "I am now."

Robbie gave a nod. "Cool. Wanna know something funny?" He walked over and flicked the back of my note cards, sending a few spiraling to the floor.

I highly doubted anything Robbie said would make me laugh right now. I was too focused on redeeming myself.

Robbie spoke anyway. "When my dad took me to meet my first celebrity at the studio, I walked around like I was some cool dude, you know, King of the World."

I raised an eyebrow. "So? You do that all the time."

He looked around as if to make sure no one was listening then leaned in and whispered, "It would have been awesome had someone told me I had this long snake-like piece of toilet paper stuck to my pants."

I laughed out loud. "Wow! That *is* embarrassing." I picked up my cards and placed them back in order. It was nice of him to try and make me smile, especially after how I had treated him the other day. "Look Robbie, I'm really sorry."

"For what?"

"For being snappy the other day. I was upset about a bunch of things. I admit, you haven't been the easiest partner to work with, but you didn't deserve me being rude."

Robbie pulled a piece of candy from his pocket. "No problemo. Apology accepted." He unwrapped it and popped it in his mouth. "So? How much you want to bet you're going to win?"

I looked Robbie square in the eye and smiled. "You just gave me a great idea."

A lady with a clipboard sprinted over when she spotted me. Kailyn straggled behind. She had walked up as Robbie and I were talking, but she refused to come over to us or make eye contact. At least she wasn't using her FBI mind-reading skills.

"Natalie Greyson?" Clipboard Lady called out.

I raised my hand. "That's me."

"And your partner, Kailyn?"

I glared at Kailyn. "Yes, my partner is Kailyn Mc-Lie-Aster."

"Excuse me?" Clipboard Lady asked, checking her list.

Kailyn made a face.

"McAllister, sorry," I repeated, like I had some brain fart.

Robbie tapped Kailyn on the shoulder, making her jump.

"Robbie! Don't do that, you scared me!" Kailyn held her hand on her chest like she was about to say The Pledge of Allegiance.

"Well you should be." He waved spirit fingers in front of her face. She swatted at them and missed. "Give up now, McAllister!"

Kailyn rolled her eyes, shifting from one foot to the next. "You're so weird."

I turned my back and headed toward the stage. As soon as my name was announced, the crowd burst into applause. Behind me, Robbie pressed something in my hand, which I fixed into the right spot. I walked in tall and proud, and hoped my shoes wouldn't squeak.

I held my head high and walked forward. I paused before I climbed the three steps and smiled toward the audience. Seconds later, the crowd's collective gasp made me turn around. Kailyn had tripped walking up the steps. She was *never* nervous, but right now her red ears stuck out of her curly hair. Quickly their gasp turned into soft laughter as they saw my last minute idea. Trailing behind me was a long piece of toilet paper, straight out of the top of my skirt. One look at Kailyn and I could see she was horrified.

Even though I could feel my face grow warm, I feigned surprise, as if I had no idea the toilet paper was there. Grabbing it and crumpling it into a ball, I turned toward the audience and giggled. "Silly me!" I said. "Oops!" I glanced over at the judges' table, and felt a surge of adrenaline when I saw Allie and Chloe grinning.

I took a seat on stage. "So, Kailyn. Welcome. Thank you for joining me today."

Kailyn squeezed her hands together. "Wouldn't have missed it."

"Great! We're all happy to have you here," I replied. Now *that* was the biggest, fattest lie of the century.

"You perform in the school talent show every year." I paused. I didn't care what Kailyn said. I was going to talk about the show during the interview. "Tell us why you are interested in being on *Kidz Konnection*."

Kailyn crossed her legs. And uncrossed them. She crossed them again, revealing her flowered, open-toed sandals. "It's always been my dream to be on TV. "

I blinked my eyes, surprised at how nervous Kailyn seemed. As I took a deep breath, ready to fire away the next question, my eyes fell on her new sandals again. They were very pretty. I bet she got them just for today.

A thought popped into my head.

"So Kailyn," I blurted out, making her jump. "Have you ever broken a bone?"

I smiled slyly. Kailyn never, *ever* wanted to talk about the foot bandage she had to wear last year. Most people thought she had broken a toe or two, but in reality she had surgery on an ingrown toenail and got a nasty toe infection. It was SO gross, I used to joke around with her that she had icky foot fungus.

"Yes. I broke a toe last year," Kailyn said frowning, her eyebrows moving toward each other like two caterpillars.

Liar liar, fungus on fire! I opened my mouth, revenge words aching to tumble out. To make her feel as awful as I did. I knew I'd catch her in a lie! And lying wasn't very professional, was it?

"Really, because I thought – " I glanced over at the judges' table. Allie and Chloe sat waiting for my response. Two best friends, maybe for eternity. I wondered if they had a Friends Forever Pact like we did; if either of them ever thought about ripping it up. But they probably never thought of embarrassing each other on stage. Best friends didn't do mean things like that.

Maybe it was the bright lights, or the fact that I had already embarrassed myself as much as I possibly could, but the realization of everything that led up to the moment hit me like a ton of bricks.

If I embarrassed Kailyn on stage, I would be just as mean as her.

I may not have gone to the exact same extremes, but my other actions were not so innocent either. And to make matters worse, I had lied to everyone, including my family, just so I could get what I wanted.

I glanced at my cards and squinted out into the audience. As far as I could tell, Mom, Dad, and the twins were missing. My thrill of a lifetime experience had not gone the way I had planned. For the first time, the audition didn't mean as much without anyone there from my family to cheer me on.

Kailyn's face was white as chalk, and her normal calm posture was now a shaky, worried mess. She pulled on one of her curls, making it bounce up and down, while glancing from me to the audience to the judges' table. Her ears were red as a tomato.

I finally let out a sigh. Deep down I knew it would be wrong for me to humiliate Kailyn. "That must have made it super hard to walk. It's impressive you were able to overcome it."

Kailyn sat up straighter. "Thank you! It was tough, but perseverance is what makes someone a star."

"Would you like to be a star one day?"

"Yes. It would be amazing to have fancy clothes and meet the coolest people." Kailyn's eyes grew wide. "Oh, and being a role model would be fantastic!"

I thought about that for a second. "Are you a role model?"

She swung her feet back and forth as she thought. I should tell her it's unprofessional, but I bit my tongue. "Yes. I totally think I am."

"What qualities do you think make someone a role model?" I asked.

Kailyn paused. "A role model is a person that is super nice to everyone and walks around confident like she is on top of the world. Everyone loves her and wants to be her."

"Do they tell secrets?" I asked.

Kailyn shook her head.

"Do they lie?"

Kailyn paused. "Well, maybe, but only if they don't want to hurt the other person's feelings. My Mom said that's called a 'white lie'."

I wanted to say that she had spouted lies during my interview. And not white lies, pink lies or any other color lies, but mean, icky ones that made me feel horrible.

"Would someone who tells *any* type of lie be a good guest host?" I asked.

Kailyn stared off into space. I knew she was reading my mind. Best friends or not, we always knew what the other one was thinking.

I glanced at my next question. Without waiting for a response, I turned toward the audience. I took a deep breath. I knew I could do this. "What do you think? If some one you knew made a mistake, you'd still like them, right?"

A chorus of "right" and "yes" traveled throughout the crowd.

Kailyn shrugged. "Well, no one is perfect, not us, not even celebrities."

I laughed. "Boy is that true! I bump microphones, have the air burps, and get toilet paper stuck in my skirt!" The audience laughed. Even the judges smiled.

With my nerves finally melting away, I launched into my finally thoughts. "I have loved this show since the very beginning. Not only is it fun and entertaining, but it inspired me to interview friends and family on my blog." I glanced over at Kailyn. "Thank you for joining me today, Kailyn. It was fabulous talking to you."

"Thank you," she replied. She glanced over at the judges' table and flashed her biggest smile.

When the audience clapped, I smiled and waved back at them like I'd seen Miss America do before, and headed off the stage. No runny noses, no stuttering, no air burps, no crying. I knew the old Kailyn would have been proud of me. The real Natalie.

And maybe my family, too, if they had seen me.

A fter all contestants held their interviews, we lined up on stage to wait for the Big Announcement. The audience quieted once Allie and Chloe joined us. I hoped it was me who would stand next to them one day.

"Thank you to everyone who came out today," Allie said. "You should all be very proud of your auditions; so many talented future talk show hosts out there!"

The crowd answered with applause.

"While Chloe and I would love to choose everyone as the winner, we can only select one." She glanced at her notes. "This person impressed us by identifying with their guest using style, humor, and wit."

I wrinkled my nose. That sounded a ton like Kailyn. Out of the corner of my eye, I noticed her look in my direction. I smiled but she quickly glanced away.

"We looked for someone who displayed tremendous courage and intelligence," Chloe said.

"The ability to interview a person in front of a crowd with ease, and has a strong passion for television. Especially *Kidz Konnection*!" Allie said, pumping her fist into the air. The audience laughed.

Aside from her lie about loving the show, how was that *not* Kailyn?

Allie continued. "The winner today surprised us with humor to lighten the mood when the situation didn't go as planned, something many of us have experienced by being on TV. A great talk show host exemplifies all those traits as well as their own fun, creative flair. Chloe and I can't wait any longer! We are very excited and happy to announce the *Kidz Konnection* guest talk show host."

"Drum roll, please!" Chloe said. The entire audience buzzed.

I sucked in my breath. Please, please let me be the next *Kidz Konnection* guest talk show host! I know I would do the best job *EVER*. Maybe better than Oprah (that's a *very* big maybe, though). I promise I will be funny and very nice to all guests.

Allie took a bright red envelope from Chloe. She looked up and smiled at the audience.

I will try not to trip or air burp on TV. And with enough practice, my Fake Shakes will disappear, poof! Like magic.

She slid her finger through the top of the envelope.

"And the winner is…."

Closing my eyes and wrapping my fingers over my acorn necklace, I sent up a silent prayer, hoping the Talk Show Goddesses had all ears open. I felt my lungs strain for air as I opened one eye to sneak a peek at Allie.

"…NATALIE GREYSON!"

As soon as my name hit my ears, it felt like a space alien had stolen my brain. I couldn't move. Couldn't talk. Couldn't think. The entire crowd gave a standing ovation.

Wahoo! I *won*. I was the *Kidz Konnection* guest talk show host!

My feet felt like they were stuck to the floor until the others next to me pushed me forward. Allie and Chloe each gave me high fives and handed me a small gold trophy molded into a big microphone. The caption underneath the microphone read: "*Kidz Konnection* Guest Talk Show Host Award." Standing there accepting my award, I felt a pang of sadness not to have my family celebrate this big moment with me.

"This microphone won't make a sound if you get too close," teased Allie. My cheeks turned pink but a giggle escaped. Some kids from my class ran up and congratulated me. Robbie came over and gave me a fist pump.

Realizing I was still holding my breath, I let out a big sigh. It came out more like a cough-grunt.

Robbie chuckled. "Nice going, Natalie! The judges must have listened to my bribes." He nudged an elbow into my ribs.

Allie and Chloe tugged on two ropes. Within seconds, I was covered in snow-like colored confetti and balloons. I twirled around and watched as the confetti flew in different directions.

Robbie turned his head toward the ceiling and stuck out his tongue long enough to catch the confetti flakes. I think he might have actually eaten a few.

All of a sudden, I felt a tap on my shoulder. When I turned around and saw who it was, I gasped in surprise.

"Grandma! What are you doing here?" She stood in front of me, a huge smile on her face and a bouquet of flowers in her arms. I gave her the biggest hug ever.

"Miss my granddaughter's on-stage debut? Never," Grandma said kissing my cheek.

I cradled the bouquet. "Daffodils," I said. "Thank you!"

"Our favorite, of course." Grandma beamed down at me.

I felt my eyes fill with tears. "I didn't think anyone was coming."

Grandma put her arm around me. "Your Mom and Dad told me how much this meant to you. They'll be so proud of you, just like I am."

"Really?" I asked. After my talk with them the other day, I didn't know they had talked about this to anyone, especially not Grandma. I wondered if she knew everything that had happened. If she did, I wasn't so sure she would be so proud of me right now.

Part of me had really wanted to tell her all about the exciting audition myself, but after all of the drama with Mom, Dad, and Kailyn, I had no energy left. Plus, deep down I knew that part of me believed I might not win.

"Of course," Grandma said. "They would have been here if the photo shoot hadn't run late. They will meet us at home." She winked at me. "You're wearing the necklace. I told you it's a lucky charm."

Allie's announcement broke through the crowd's loud chatter. "We'd like everyone to join us in the conference meeting room around the corner for snacks and refreshments!"

As I made my way there, it was like I was already a celebrity. Moms and dads and little brothers and sisters came up and congratulated me. I said "thank you" so many times, I felt like I was a robot with a vocabulary of two words. Even when Mrs. Wayne asked how I felt, I answered with a "thank you".

A large banner with the word "CONGRATULATIONS!" hung over the conference room doors. Red, black, and gold balloons (*Kidz Konnection* colors, of course!) decorated the centers of each table. Allie and Chloe spotted me right away and waved me over. Butterflies swirled in my stomach. They wanted to talk to *me*.

"Congrats again, Natalie," they said together. They looked at each other and laughed.

"Go grab some treats and then come sit with us," Chloe said.

I grinned. Somebody pinch me. This was what I had dreamed about!

The refreshment table was like a dream come true. I couldn't have asked for better treats if I had a genie in a bottle who granted me one wish. Fudge brownies, cupcakes with red, black, and yellow oozing icing and sprinkles, cookies with gigantic size chocolate and peanut butter chips (my absolute favorite!) with the words WAY TO GO! and KIDZ KONNECTION written out on them, and ice cream with a bazillion toppings to choose from. The coolest part was the SUPER HUGE triple layer cake. Half of it was sparkly gold with ribbons of white icing, while the other was red with black swirls of icing.

I made sure to take a little bit of everything.

Juggling a plate sky-high with baked treats, a BIG piece of cake, and a scoop of ice cream, I tried to make it to my seat without spilling, while Grandma sat with some of the other adults.

"You're going to love being a guest host, Natalie," Allie said, once I sat down.

Chloe squeezed my arm. "Next Saturday is a big day! You'll come to the studio where we'll show you around, introduce you to everyone, the whole shebang. There will be a small party afterwards, too." She leaned in and whispered, "If you're lucky maybe a celebrity will already be in the studio!"

Allie ate a spoonful of ice cream. "Don't forget you can bring some friends too if you'd like."

Suddenly, as I took in the scene around me, I wasn't hungry any more. Every part of me knew I should be excited—no, *beyond* excited—about winning. But I hated not being able to celebrate this moment with the rest of my family. On top of that, my best friend wanted nothing to do with me. I had finally reached my dream. But I was starting to realize what it had cost me.

Saturday, April 22
Logged on IN A NAT SHELL
(*via Oak Grove Elementary Intranet*) **at 7:12 PM:**

Hello everyone!

This is my VERY FIRST blog post as . . . (drumroll!) THE GUEST HOST OF *KIDZ KONNECTION*!!!

I can't WAIT for the day I get to interview celebrities! So, the past couple weeks have been, well as my friends would say "nutty." And with me being the guest host, I have a feeling it's about to get a bit nuttier! (I wonder if that can be my signature saying or something? I'll have to think about it some more. Let me know if you have any neat ideas).

Stay tuned for more updates! You don't want to miss any of it!

"Time to shine!"

That's me In A Nat Shell,

Natalie

TAKE 17

hat up, Reality Natalie?" Robbie chanted as I walked into the classroom the following Monday. "Got a nice ring to it, don't ya think?"

I nodded. "Not bad."

Robbie lightly punched me on the arm. "Now I can say I know another celebrity." He leaned forward and whispered, "But let me know if you ever see toilet paper stuck to my shoe or something. Got it?"

I smiled. "Will do."

Glancing around the room, I noticed everyone getting their presentations ready. I was glad that Robbie and I decided to split up the final work. I put the finishing touches on mine last night. I had asked Mom if I could have coffee to sip while finishing my project, thinking it would be like Talk-Show-Host-Drinking-Coffee practice. She said I'd be bouncing off the walls like a rubber ball if I had coffee, so she gave me hot chocolate with extra marshmallows instead.

Kailyn sat in the back with her partner, staring off into space. I was about to go talk to her when Mrs. Wayne whistled for everyone to sit.

One group volunteered to go first. My thoughts drifted back to Saturday and the moment I was announced as the winner.

It was the best time in my life. When Grandma and I arrived home, Mom, Dad, and the twins were there with flowers and a cake. Sydney and Chase had even made a banner that spelled "Congratulations" for me in lots of colors. But despite my excitement, Kailyn kept invading my thoughts. What I wanted was to jump up and down with her and Maggie and make up fun questions for the celebrity guests.

"Natalie, you're next," Mrs. Wayne said, waving me to the front of the classroom.

Whoa, déjà vu. But this time, I walked up with my shoulders straight.

"Robbie Lovelton, too," Mrs. Wayne added.

"Our topic is fear," I said. I took a deep breath and looked around the room. The entire class stared. At me. For a moment, I thought I felt a flutter in my stomach. I closed my eyes and counted to three. When I opened them again, everyone was still staring at me. But this time, I had no cherry red face, no runny nose, no Fake Shakes, no air burps.

I took a deep breath and decided to pose a question to the class. "Has anyone ever been afraid of anything?"

People glanced around at each other. Finally, Megan raised her hand. "I'm afraid of spiders." She paused. "Well, at least the ones that aren't dead."

Others began to chime in.

"I'm afraid of sharks."

"I don't like heights one bit."

"Snakes scare me to death!"

"I'm afraid every time my grandma pinches my cheek!"

Everyone laughed.

I continued, "Many people think fear is talking about being afraid of something—like a dog or the dark or scary movies. But it can be anything."

I looked around the room. Everyone's eyes were glued to me.

"I realized I am a lot like Amelia Earhart. Even though I was afraid to try something new and scary, like auditioning for the *Kidz Konnection* guest host position in front of strangers despite my fear of the stage, I knew I would do my best if I worked hard enough and *believed* I could do it. And didn't let my fears get in the way. Amelia didn't care what others thought, and she flew across the entire ocean! " I paused and looked at my notes. "I might have to add flying over the ocean to my list of Things To Do."

The class laughed, even Mrs. Wayne.

Afterwards, I helped Robbie with the next part of our presentation. He chose three students to come up and guess what might be in one of three mystery boxes. We rated how scared they were to close their eyes and have us place the object on their hand. (All the boxes contained a normal object like candy or a pen). As Robbie's idea, I had to admit it was a pretty cool presentation about overcoming fear. He tried to crack (somewhat) funny jokes, and I was glad the kids were laughing at his craziness rather than my silly air burps.

Before I knew it, we had finished our presentation. Mrs. Wayne and the class clapped as we walked back to our seats.

Robbie gave me a high-five. "Good job, partner!"

"Thanks," I said. "I think everyone enjoyed it."

Robbie snorted. "Duh, because I'm one awesome entertainer!" He flung one of his legs onto the seat next to him and flexed his muscles like he was a body-builder.

I groaned. Some things never changed. I sat at my desk, while Robbie continued to flex his arms in various positions.

"Boys and girls, before we continue with our presentations, I'd like to announce some exciting news. As everyone knows, I'm very proud to announce that the *Kidz Konnection* guest host contest winner is our very own, Natalie Greyson," Mrs. Wayne said. Her black and gold bangle bracelets clanged together as she clapped along with the class.

I turned to smile at my classmates. Out of the corner of my eye, I saw Kailyn clapping half-heartedly. As soon as our eyes met, she looked away. I bit my lower lip. Maybe she was mad I didn't talk with her after the audition. I couldn't tell for sure, but I hoped to find out soon.

"In honor of this tremendous occasion, I brought in some cookies and refreshments to celebrate. Natalie, would you like to help pass them out?" Mrs. Wayne held out the plastic container of cookies in my direction. "I'll pour the lemonade for everyone."

I leaped out of my seat, took the container from her, and grabbed a stack of napkins. At each desk, I tried to give my classmates my best TV star smile. Some of them smiled back, while others didn't pay attention. Before I knew it, I was at Kailyn's desk.

"Oh, hey Kailyn." I placed a napkin on her desk. "Do you want a cookie?"

Kailyn nodded. I dug into the container to grab one, but I must have been too quick. The plastic container teetered in my hands, sending a few cookies flying straight toward the floor. Bits and pieces spotted Kailyn's black flats.

"Natalie! I just *bought* these," Kailyn cried, brushing off the tops of her shoes.

I bent down and picked up the broken pieces. "Sorry! It was an accident."

"Not to worry, I have another box in case we don't have enough," Mrs. Wayne said, hustling down the aisle, her tights swishing together as she moved. After we cleaned up the crumbs, and the entire class had a cookie, I bit into mine. Except by now, the cookie tasted like cardboard, making me nauseous. Kailyn was definitely still mad at me. I had a feeling it wasn't because of my "cookie crisis" either.

If Kailyn was going to be like that, let her have her way. If she didn't want to be best friends, fine. I still had Maggie.

But a small thought crept into my mind. Without Kailyn *and* our pact, would the Divine Girls be over for good?

TAKE 18

The week flew by, and Kailyn and I still were not talking. She clearly avoided me whenever she could. Maggie wasn't happy about the fight, but said she didn't want to get in the middle. She told me in private that she figured Kailyn would come around soon but just needed time.

By Thursday evening, I still had a giant pit in my stomach. The kind you get when you don't want to go to school because you didn't finish your homework, or you fear The Big Test. I would have kissed a slimy spotted toad for any of those to be my biggest problem right now.

Kailyn and I hadn't talked once since Monday. No email, no blog comment, no phone call; zip, zero, zilch. Tomorrow was the TV studio party, and I still hadn't asked her if she wanted to come. I knew I should at least try calling her, but part of me was afraid she'd think I was bragging about the party.

Even though I could tell my family was happy for me, something felt wrong. If I was ever going to enjoy this moment, I needed to make things right, starting with them. Rolling my shoulders back and standing tall, I marched down to the living room where Mom and Dad watched TV on the couch.

I cleared my throat. "Uh, Mom? Dad? Can I talk to you?"

Both of them looked my direction and patted the seat next to them. I inched closer but stayed standing.

"I want to say I'm sorry. For everything. I was wrong to take matters into my own hands." I tried to fight back the tears welling up. "If I could go back in time, I would do things differently. I know that now."

Mom looked at Dad, then back at me. "Thank you for the apology."

"Can you tell us why you thought it was okay to lie?" Dad asked. "Did you think we wouldn't find out?"

"I don't know! I guess I didn't think that far ahead. Everything was so, so messed up. Robbie was being the world's worst partner, I really thought we'd get an F, no an F minus. Mrs. Wayne would have needed to invent another grade worse than F. Then you guys said I couldn't try out for the audition, but Kailyn was, and I just couldn't let her win another thing. So when we practiced, she was a gigantic Mean Queen!" I knew I was starting to sound like a blubbering mess but I continued anyway. "Can you believe she ripped up our friendship pact? And she embarrassed me on stage. I don't even know if we're best friends any more. No best friend would ever do the things she did." Tears streamed down my face.

Mom leaned over, grabbed a tissue from the coffee table and handed it to me.

"But I guess that's fine. I don't need—a—bossy—friend—anyway," I said through gulps of air.

Mom sighed, put down her Soduku puzzle, and held my hand. "I'm glad you realize just how many sacrifices went into this audition of yours. It's evidently caused a lot of hurt feelings with Kailyn, and around here as well."

I nodded, sniffling.

"I should admit, we honestly didn't take this as seriously as we should have. You change your mind so often, we didn't think this would be any different."

"No, I wanted this more than *anything* in the world." I dug my toe into the carpet. "But it wasn't worth it if it meant losing my best friend." I paused and took a deep breath. "And it is definitely not worth it if you guys don't trust me anymore."

Mom and Dad gave each other "the look" again.

Dad spoke up. "Yes, we were very disappointed in the way you handled the situation. You lied to us, went behind our backs, and forged a signature without our permission. Trust is earned not given. Hopefully the past couple weeks have shown you that. But no matter what, we'll always encourage you to go after what you are passionate about because we love you."

"Not as much as the twins," I muttered. "I overheard you talking last week about me being too young for the show."

Mom looked confused. "Well, you must have heard wrong then. We were talking about the twins and what was best for them at the time. It had nothing to do with you or the show."

Darn. Leave it to me to assume things.

"Natalie, what you didn't seem to realize was how much was given up for you in the past," Dad said. "How many times we all had to give up our Saturday mornings to drive you to your gymnastics practices, or attend your dance recitals –"

"...don't forget the school play," Mom added. "And choir concerts and singing lessons."

Dad nodded. "Sometimes there are going to be times when we just cannot do it all. There will be disappointing moments, but we do the best we can as a family, and that's something you will have to learn to accept."

"There will always be other opportunities," Mom said. "So if things don't go your way, it's not because we don't want to see you succeed or that we don't support you."

"The twins were sad you weren't at their photo shoot," Dad explained. "They wanted their big sister there, someone they look up to. They have been there for you a lot, and you could have been there for them for a change."

Mom got up from the couch. "I have something to show you." When she came back a few seconds later, she held her camera. She stopped on a picture and handed it to me. My siblings smiled at the camera, both decked out in colorful clothes. They held a small sign in-between them.

"Obviously, I had to take some of my own pictures of the photo shoot," Mom said. "I think you'll like that one a lot."

I zoomed in closer to see what the sign said. *Our sister is our star.*

It's like that feeling when you have a bad cold, and all of a sudden the time comes when you can breathe again. For the first time in a long while, I finally had clarity. What I should have seen ages ago. I knew Mom and Dad were right. I may not have been as cunning as Kailyn was during our interview, but I certainly hadn't been a best friend or the world's greatest daughter or sister either. To get what I wanted I hurt a lot of people's feelings and lost their trust.

"Wow. That means a lot. I can't believe they thought of me," I said, handing the camera back to Mom. "I never meant for any of this to happen. I guess all I could think about was becoming Natalie Greyson – 'the talk show host'." I looked upward as if I already saw my name lit up in lights. I shrugged. "I feel awful. I was completely selfish. I ditched our family photo shoot, lied to you both, and my best friend and I aren't speaking." I paused. "I have lost more than I won."

Finally saying it all out loud made it sound even worse. Despite everything I did, people had still been there for me in some way. Grandma had come to support me, and the twins were thoughtful enough to think of me during *their* shining moment.

"You did the right thing by coming to us and apologizing. And it seems you've learned a lesson or two through all of this," Dad said. "Maybe it's not too late for you and Kailyn. After all, you guys are best friends. She may understand where you were coming from."

I thought about that for a second. "What if she doesn't understand? What if she doesn't want to be best friends anymore?"

"No fear, right?" Dad said, winking. "Besides, you'll never know unless you try."

* * * * *

The next morning before school, I pulled the twins aside and apologized for my behavior. Either they were too young to understand or they happen to be the most forgiving siblings on Earth, but both of them gave me hugs and kisses. Regardless, I promised them I would make more of an effort to be a better, supportive sister, and told them I'd hang their sign in my room.

On the bus, I was determined to fix what happened between Kailyn and me. If I could make things better with my family, why couldn't I with my best friend, too? I took out a piece of paper and pen and brainstormed ways on how to get the three of us back together as best friends:

1. Throw a surprise Divine Girls party with lots and lots of chocolate
2. Bake Kailyn's favorite dessert
3. Ask Allie and Chloe if there can be a second guest host

I scrunched up my nose. Not horrible ideas but none of them promised Kailyn would stop being mad. Plus, as much as I knew friends shared things, I was super proud of winning the guest host spot and wasn't too sure about sharing. It would never work. The spot was for one person.

Too bad I couldn't go back in time. A time warping machine would be fantastic. Then I could go back, and Kailyn and I would practice our questions together with NO fighting and redo the real interviews so we *both* rocked them fair and square.

Maybe we'd be so impressive, they'd have to accept both of us as guest hosts.

A thought popped into my head. That was it!

In order for my plan to work, I had to talk to Maggie. I scribbled down some notes, excited to get to school and put my plan into action.

Take that, Pit of Worry! The Divine Girls were going to unite again!

TAKE 19

When I got to class, I tossed my jacket over my chair and made a beeline for Maggie's desk. I forced my feet to come to a complete halt, almost tripping over nothing as Kailyn skipped over to Maggie and whispered something into her ear. Was she talking about me? As if she heard my thoughts, Kailyn glanced in my direction.

Mrs. Wayne whistled and called everyone to their desks. No time to talk to Maggie about my plan.

"Class, this morning we're going to start our day with a spelling pre-test," Mrs. Wayne said. "Maggie, will you please pass out some blank paper?"

Before Maggie stood, Kailyn tapped her on the shoulder and passed a note. Maggie read it and covered her mouth with her hand, stifling a giggle. My stomach flip-flopped. My mind traveled back to when I used to play the Note Passing Game, too. Sometimes we'd make a super-fun bet. If Mrs. Wayne caught you passing a note, you'd have to bring tasty treats to lunch the following day.

I scribbled my own note to Maggie:

Emergency!!
Divine Girls Revival meeting tonight.
Meet at the clubhouse – 5 pm sharp!

When no spies were watching, I handed it to Maggie as she passed by, making sure this time she actually got it. She sat and read my note. Seconds later she glanced my way and gave me a thumbs-up sign.

I grinned and sat tall in my chair, feeling super confident. It was time to put my plan into action.

* * * * *

After school, Maggie and I waited for our guest to arrive at our clubhouse. The butterflies in my stomach fluttered like crazy. I couldn't decide if they were worse today or during my real audition for *Kidz Konnection*. I peeked through the peephole facing the house. Nothing.

"Maybe she won't show up," I said, chewing on a fingernail. "What if she saw me coming through her backyard?" I scanned the colored note cards in my hands for the millionth time. Each one had a different question on them. Even though I wrote them during lunch and thought of awesome answers for Maggie, Now my mind was going blank.

Maggie shook her head and popped a marshmallow into her mouth. "Nah. She'll be here. She still has exactly one minute and thirty-two seconds. Otherwise she will be fashionably late."

"Interesting," I said. "And yet, she gave me such a hard time for being three minutes late for practice. That's not being 'professional and prepared' now, is it?"

"Shh!" Maggie said, smiling and lightly swatting at me. She squinted through the peephole. "Here she comes!" She took the cards from my hands and grabbed a round hairbrush from her backpack.

With every sound of Kailyn's steps on the ladder, my heart beat faster. Maggie handed me a tissue. "Here. Just in case." She smiled. "Rock it out, Nats!"

Kailyn popped through the door. As soon as she saw me, her smile faded. "What are *you* doing here?"

Maggie cleared her throat, glanced at her cards, and spoke an octave higher than normal into the hairbrush.

"Kailyn McAllister, welcome to the first live version of the *Divine Girls Clubhouse Show*! I'm your host, Maggie Castlebury, and this is our guest, Natalie Greyson. Please take a seat."

Kailyn glanced from Maggie to me several times before plopping down on a pillow across from me and crossing her arms. "What's going on?"

"It has come to our attention that the Divine Girls are *Not*-So-Divine anymore. Kailyn, would you please explain to our guest here why you are so mad?"

Kailyn eyed both of us warily. "*Natalie* knows why," she said.

"Does she?" Maggie asked. "But can you inform the audience why?"

Kailyn frowned and looked around. "What audience?" She paused as if thinking. "Anyway, I didn't expect my very own best friend to embarrass me in front of the entire school about my broken toe."

"First of all, it was NOT a broken toe," I blurted out, "and I stopped before I went any further. Second of all, you're the one that embarrassed me when you brought up how klutzy and unprofessional I am."

"You're just being overly sensitive," Kailyn said with a slight shrug.

I felt the heat crawl up my neck like fire ants. "You lied about the cake. That never happened. And the incident at the studio with the microphone—you knew that was an accident."

"Excuse me girls, can we—" Maggie interrupted.

Kailyn raised an eyebrow. "You are one to talk! You lied first about "meeting" Allie!" she said, using air quotes.

My mind buzzed like angry bumblebees. "I was forced to! I had no choice. *You* did!"

"Girls, come on," Maggie said, clearing her throat.

"Oh yeah?" Kailyn asked.

"You didn't tell me you had changed your questions, especially to talk about the show. *And* you lied about loving it. I doubt you've even seen one episode." I shook my head. A marshmallow bounced off my cheek, and I absentmindedly rubbed at the spot.

"I told you to prepare. I decided to change my questions after seeing how the other interviews went. Anyone else would have. What's the big deal?" Kailyn said.

I crossed my arms. "Big deal? Guess I forgot that you aced "How Not to Be A Best Friend 101.""

"You're just jealous because I'm talented, and everyone knows it." Kailyn stood at the same moment a marshmallow hit her arm. Seconds later, another hit her square on the nose.

"Ohhhh girls..." Maggie sang. "The host is getting bored."

"*That's* what they call talent these days?" I retorted.

Kailyn glared at me. "Whatever, Miss Robzilla Lover!"

"Toenail Fungus Queen!"

"Nasty Nose Runner!"

"Miss Bossy Bonehead!"

"HEY!" Maggie yelled.

Kailyn and I turned in unison toward her and yelled, "WHAT?"

"I think, as your best friend, I should warn you that you both are under attack from the marshmallow martians!" She chucked handfuls of marshmallows right at our faces, over and over again. "They won't stop! Take cover!" It was a marshmallow bombing; all of us started shrieking with laughter.

I screamed and tried to duck, but it was too late. Two marshmallows bounced off my face, and one more ricocheted off my leg. I looked up just in time to see Maggie toss a few at Kailyn. She squealed and shielded her head with her arms. "Stop, stop already!" she pleaded, a few giggles breaking through.

"Not until you bozos stop fighting," Maggie said, reaching into the plastic bag for more ammo.

"But she hasn't apologized!" I said. Before I could say more, another marshmallow bomb hit me on the forehead.

"You *both* should apologize." Maggie squinted her eyes at Kailyn. "I believe both of you broke a Divine Girl's rule: be honest and not keep anything from each other. Plus, you almost broke another: keep each other's secrets."

Nobody said anything for a whole five seconds. Maggie did have a point. Best friends do not spill each other's secrets, nor keep any from them. That was not being honest or fair. We were both guilty as charged.

Kailyn diverted her eyes from me to the floor before finally speaking. "Guess I wasn't Divine Girls material, huh?"

I felt a small tug at my heart. "Yea. Me, either," I said flipping a marshmallow with my toe.

"I'm sorry, Natalie. It's just…I dunno…I guess I *was* jealous you were trying out for TV, not something small and lame like the talent show. So I decided to as well. And then when you won, and I didn't…" She shrugged.

"I'm sorry, too. But you know what? I'm always jealous of you!" I said.

Kailyn raised her eyebrows. "Really? Jealous of what?"

"You win the talent show almost every year. You are the best singer I know. Nobody stands a chance going up against you. You are so cool." I paused. "And I lied about a lot of things. My parents actually said 'no' to me trying out, at first."

"They did? You never said anything," Kailyn said. "But I'm glad they decided to let you. You deserved to win. I was wrong to make up things about you in front of everyone."

"Well, I wasn't much better. I was a crazy person the past couple weeks, Kailyn. All I thought about was the audition, and part of me forgot what being a best friend was all about. I should have been more supportive of you trying out, too," I said. "I realized that getting the chance to try out made me feel, even for just a second, what it feels like to be, well, you."

"Nats, you're going to be on TV! Like a *real* celebrity. I never got that far."

I grabbed her hand. "Listen, I'm sorry I posted that comment on my blog. Yes, I wanted to win, but if you had won, you would have been a fantastic guest host, I know it."

Kailyn threw her arms around my neck in a big hug.

I squeezed my best friend back. "I'd love it if you came to the studio party with me and Maggie tomorrow. I want you to be a part of it, too. It wouldn't be the same without you there."

"You do? After everything that happened between us?" Kailyn asked.

I nodded. "We can put on sunglasses and feather boas and our best heels and maybe even some makeup and act like real celebrities!"

Maggie faked a cough and waved the hairbrush microphone in front of us. "Um, hello, I thought *I* was the host ..."

Kailyn and I laughed.

"Sorry, Mag-Pie," I said, putting an arm around her shoulder. "Looks like the Divine Girls are back in business!" I took the hairbrush from Maggie and thrust my arm into the air.

"Hurray!" all three of us said in unison.

"This is another huge moment," I said.

"Biggest. Moment. Ever. We should do something to mark it," Maggie replied. "Again—ha!"

"I have an idea." Kailyn rummaged around in the treasure chest and pulled out scrap pieces of paper and some tape. "Let's make it an even better one." She looked at both of us and smiled.

Looking closer, the pieces of paper weren't scrap sheets, but the old pact Kailyn had ripped up. She put them together like a puzzle and taped it. "What should we add?"

I grabbed a pen from the table and after thinking for a couple of seconds, I wrote down my idea:

5. Never let ANYTHING in the ENTIRE blue and green world come between the Divine Girls!

"Done-zo!" I said, glancing at my work.

Kailyn and Maggie peered over my shoulder.

"Perfect-o!" Kailyn said. "Definitely what I was thinking!"

"Neat-o skeet- o!" Maggie replied.

All of us took turns signing our names.

"Hey, bird brains!"

"Who is that?" Maggie said. She ran to the window and looked out the peephole. "Oh it's Jesse."

Kailyn groaned. "What does he want? Doesn't he know we are in the middle of a Top Secret Divine Girls meeting?" She walked over to the window. "What do you want, Jesse!" she yelled down to her older brother.

"It's dinnertime! It's your turn to set the table. Mom said your bird-brain friends can stay."

"Maybe we should add something else to the pact," I grumbled, after Jesse had walked away. "Hide spiders in our brothers' beds."

"Or red ants in their shoes," Kailyn added.

"But wouldn't that be breaking number one of our pact?" Maggie asked. "Be nice to our siblings?"

All three of us went silent.

"Eh, who cares? We're making a better pact, right?" Kailyn blurted out. "And brothers stink!" She picked up the pen and scribbled over number one.

The Divine Girls, united again, burst into laughter.

Saturday, April 29
Logged on IN A NAT SHELL
(*via Oak Grove Elementary Intranet*) at 9:48 PM:

Hello world!!

I have GREEEATTTTT EXCITING (and a little sad!) news to share. Today at the *Kidz Konnection* studio party, I found out that Allie Marks is LEAVING (yes, leaving) the show soon! She will be starring in a new movie called RACE TO SPACE.

CONGRATULATIONS TO ALLIE!!

However, this means they will need to find another PER-MANENT host to take her spot.

Crossing all ten fingers and all ten toes that maybe, just maybe, I will get the job! What do you think??

That's me in a Brand *New* Nat Shell,
Natalie

Shared Comments:

Logged on IN A NAT SHELL at 10:19 PM

Hail2KailGal: CONGRATS!!!!!!! You're famous!

Logged on IN A NAT SHELL at 10:42 PM

MagPie54: So excited!! Yay Nats!! Can I get your auto-graph? :)

Logged on IN A NAT SHELL at 11:05 PM

Robzilla200007: Ribbit!

I logged out of my blog and clicked my computer shut. Leaning back in my purple chair, I thought about everything that happened in the past month. Who would have thought I would get to be a guest host on my favorite talk show? I wondered which celebrities I would interview. And now with Allie leaving, would I have the chance to become *more* than a guest host?

I rubbed my acorn necklace and smiled. With Kailyn and Maggie as my best friends, I knew it was only going to get so much better.

That's a wrap!

ABOUT THE AUTHOR

At a very young age, Katie Sparks discovered the magic of books. She counted on weekly library visits and treasured receiving her first library card at the age of five. At six, she wrote her first story called *Baby Carrie* (still in her collection today!) Katie knew then that writing would be in her future. By day, she is an editor for the parent consumer line at a non-profit medical association and enjoys working closely with authors and industry professionals. Immersed in the publishing industry in both her professional and personal life is a dream come true. On weekends you will often find her writing and sipping coffee at one of the many unique coffee shops in Chicago, spending time with family and friends, or curled up with a new book.

Katie has been an active member of SCBWI for the past seven years. She lives in Chicago with her devoted and extremely vocal cat Moe. *Reality Natalie,* is her first novel.

THANKS!

We often hear that writing a book is a very isolating activity. However, I would not be in this wonderful position right now if it weren't for so many important people in my life. First and foremost, thank you to God. I believe I was born in this world to do something amazing, and I truly hope it was to touch children's lives with the written word.

To my Wednesday night Barnes and Noble critique groups. What would I do without you all? Not only have you shaped my manuscripts into successful stories, but you have also shaped me into a stronger, solid writer. To my two writing partners in crime – Kym Brunner and Cherie Colyer. Kym– I still remember you calling me after my first critique group, afraid that I might have gotten scared off and asking me if I would come back. Seven years later, I'm still here! With your guidance, I haven't lost my way. (Just follow the blue dot, right?) Cherie – I'm so glad that you're not only a critique buddy, but a good friend. Your talent shines on the page, and I'm so glad I have been able to witness it firsthand and learn from you. Especially being your assistant at the wine and cheese party. ☺

Not enough thanks can be extended to my other writing group cheerleaders: Veronica Rundell, Terri Murphy, Mike Kelly, Susan Kaye Quinn, Marian Cheatham, Terry Flamm, Meg Lenz, Allan Woodrow, and many more. Thank you for all of your honest input and advice. Because of you guys "Natalie" is now a "reality." To SCBWI (and friends!) for being such a wonderful organization for writers and illustrators, guiding us along the path to achieving our dream. I am honored to be a part of this inspiring group of talented people. I'd be remiss if I didn't send a special shout out to Mat Raney for being an honest beta reader when I needed the brutal truth!

To my editor and publisher, Nikki Bennett. I'm truly honored to be a part of Firedrake Books. Without your vision and passion, "Reality Natalie" would not have come alive. You have made my dream come true.

Hugs and kisses also to Rebecca, "Woman", Christy "Twinny", Michelle "Smurph" and all of my BDUB girls from ISU. To my high school and Chicago friends who have never left my side, Jessica "Natterz", Lauren "Cinny", Erica (Go Bears!), Nikki, Jaime, Liz and Amy; thank you for understanding all of the times when I had to say no to plans so I could write. Or edit. Or revise. Then write some more.

A big heartfelt thanks to Mike Durr, who has a talented and creative eye when it comes to photography. Thank you for the best author photos ever! (www.michaeldurr. com folks!)

To my sister Jen – you've been my most enthusiastic fan. This is the most thrilling time in my life and from the beginning you've always been right alongside me just as excited. To be able to share this moment with you is incredible. Sisters are best friends we are born with. Thank you for being someone I can look up to, trust, and love unconditionally.

Huge shout-outs to Stacey "BIL", the world's best nephew, Parker, and Lindsay "SIL" --I'm so grateful to have you all in my life.

To my twin, Steve --"Brother" – Thanks for always being my partner in crime, then and now. You've always encouraged me to "do better" whether it was being a soccer goalie, a hackey sack pro (you know I am) or in my writing career. You've always had my back.

To my grandparents, Bette and Hank, 'Cuz' Dan, Uncle Rick, Aunt Jill, Regina and Tommy – I'm truly honored to have you as my biggest supporters, but also as my family.

Last, but certainly, not least --to my Mom – aka, Mi Ma, Madre, or Mush – You are my rock. My biggest cheerleader. My world. I'm 100% convinced I fell in love with books and writing because of you. Thank you for always cheering for me regardless of where I was in the game, and when I reached the end, you congratulated me, hugged me and told me "It's just the beginning." I hope I make you proud.

CPSIA information can be obtained
at www.ICGtesting.com
Printed in the USA
LVOW04s1004280216

477035LV00015B/683/P